DEDICATION

Dedicated to the music of Depeche Mode,
the artwork of Sandy DeLuca, and the
memory of Joe McKinney.

WAITING FOR THE NIGHT

A
GRINNING SKULL PRESS
Publication

WAITING FOR THE NIGHT

by Michael McCarty & Terrie Leigh Relf

CONTENTS

ACKNOWLEDGMENTS

Michael McCarty

My lovely wife, Cindy McCarty, my good friend and writing partner Terrie Leigh Relf, Michael Evans, Harrison Graves, and the staff of Grinning Skull Press, Bruce Walters, Sandy DeLuca, Rodney & Amanda McNeill, Kristin DeMarr, The McCartys, The Hultings, The Leonards, The Thompsons, The Beach Party Zombies, Mel Piff, Jack, Camilla, Holly, Brian, Sarah Holderfield, Bruce Cook, Sam & Kathy Paddie, Joe Collins, Nancy Johnston, Char, R.L. Fox, Stuart Mesmer, Andy Masengarb, Ray Bradbury, Dean Koontz, William F. Nolan, Mark Allan Gunnells, Richard Laymon, H.P. Lovecraft, Edgar Allan Poe, Joe Hill, Cherie Day, Obsidian & Sage, The Brewed Book, Lynn and Barnes & Noble, The Book Rack, Veronique Fernandez, Shannon Trimble, the memory of my parents Bev and Gerald, Yeti and the memory of Kitty and Latte and all my family and friends and fans—you are the reason I keep writing.

Terrie Leigh Relf

I want to first thank my writing partner, Michael McCarty, for asking me to participate in what I believe will be an awesome collection! Secondly, I want to thank all the editors who have published my work in the past as well as in the future. Thirdly, I want to thank everyone who has read and will continue to read my work. Fourthly, of course, I thank everyone who has inspired and mentored me throughout my career, including my two podlings, Brandon and Willow.

INTRODUCTION:
WELCOME TO THE NIGHT

I've read *Waiting for the Night: Dark and Strange Tales* by Michael McCarty and Terrie Leigh Relf, and it's been a treat. It goes without saying, I was honored when asked to write the introduction for these two authors.

I've collaborated with Michael on various pieces of fiction and poetry over the years, and I've had the pleasure of contributing my art as covers for his books on occasion. I first met him at a World Horror Convention decades ago. Even back then, I appreciated his humor, his intelligence, and dedication to the genre. His interviews are legendary. His fiction and poetry are rich with wit and originality.

I've known Terrie for many years as well. She's edited various publications I've contributed to, and I worked with her on one occasion, along with Marge Simon, on a cookbook. That's right! A cookbook! *The Intergalactic Cookbook.* Her imagination is boundless, giving her the ability to create exotic worlds—to delineate memorable characters. It's no wonder that when these two combined their talents, they came up with a treasure such as *Waiting for the Night.* It's an exquisite collaborative assemblage. Here, you'll find staples of genre fiction—vampires, zombies, ghosts, werewolves, and aliens. They exist, but they—and their stories—are packed with unique punches and twists. The endings are not always predictable; sometimes, settings and universes are quite unusual as well. Some are written in partnership—seamlessly and brilliantly. The writers have gone solo on others. Relf paints exotic worlds and beings. McCarty doesn't hold back on his special blend of darkness.

After all these years, it's always a kick to discover new talent and ideas. However, familiar voices that have resonated after decades of hard work and effort are often the best treats for fans of dark and imaginative fiction.

I hope you enjoy the thrills and surprises as much as I have.

—Sandy DeLuca, June 12th, 2023

COLLABORATIVE STORIES

HELP WANTED

Five o'clock finally arrived, and Roberta Cannon smiled for the first time that Friday. It had been a hectic week, and all she wanted to do now was go home, strip off her office clothes, take a long, hot bath, drink a lite beer, and watch TV with her live-in boyfriend, Kevin VanZant.

She had just finished typing her last invoice and was ready to shut off her computer, swipe her timecard, go home, and not think about work until Monday morning at 8 a.m. when her alarm clock would go off. That was a nice thought—putting work out of her mind completely—but she knew that was impossible, since her boyfriend worked as the shipping manager.

Siralop Appliances was all too often the topic of their conversations when they talked. Most of the time, they sat in silence watching the tube or crawled all over each other in bed. And when they did speak to each other, it would be a bitch-fest about work.

Files saved so she could continue typing invoices on Monday morning, Roberta thought about how summer was their busiest time of year—more invoices, more files. She grabbed her purse, took out her timecard, and then Charlene Maltins tapped her on the shoulder.

Charlene, a twenty-something blonde, had flunked out of college her freshman year and had a smile as phony as her overly padded bra. Her slender finger tapped Roberta lightly on the shoulder, but it still made her skin crawl.

"Like, Mister Krall wants to see you." Charlene popped her stale strawberry bubble gum, some of which stuck to what appeared to be glossy collagen-enhanced lips. Hands on hips, she studied Roberta, looking her up and down, her dark indigo eyes lingering too long on the older woman's body. "He wanted me to tell you earlier, but it slipped my mind. I saw you coming toward the time clock, and then I remembered."

"It's five o'clock. Can't it wait until Monday morning?" Roberta said, more than a bit peeved. Ever since Charlene had started working here, it was all Roberta could do to refrain from yelling at her, "Get a brain already!" She straightened her skirt, stroking the thin fabric around her hips. This did not go unnoticed by Charlene.

Charlene, who was Mr. Krall's secretary, scrunched up her pretty face and appeared to think about Roberta's question for a moment. "He said it was *really* important, and to tell you before you left for the day." She studied Roberta's body again, frowned, then brightened as if she'd finally had an idea worth mentioning.

"I bet you have to work out a lot to keep the flab off," she smirked, tossing her hair like the cliché she was, before pivoting on her sandals and sashaying down the hall.

Roberta sighed. Charlene wasn't worth getting worked up over. How she longed for that hot bath, cold beer, TV—and especially Kevin—but all that would have to wait.

She entered Mr. Krall's small office, which consisted of a desk, phone, computer, two chairs by the wall, and seven filing cabinets. Mr. Krall himself was a pudgy, fifty-something bald man who never smiled the whole six weeks Roberta had been working at Siralop Appliances.

"Have a seat," Mr. Krall said, pointing to the first chair against the wall.

Roberta sat down and smoothed a crease in her skirt.

Mr. Krall pulled out a file and studied its contents for two minutes before speaking. "You've been working here for six weeks, is that correct, Miz Cannon?"

"Yes."

"I hired you because of the recommendation from Mister Van-Zant. And so far, there haven't been any complaints. You've been a fine worker—so far." He paused, put down the file, and looked Roberta directly in the eyes. "Miz Cannon, Siralop Appliances is a small business, and the employees in small businesses are almost like family members. In any family, trust is very important. Wouldn't you agree?"

Roberta felt like a cornered animal. *Maybe he knows*, she thought. But there was no way that her scheme with Kevin could have backfired. Still, she couldn't shake the feeling that something wasn't right here. She looked anxiously at the door, then returned her gaze to Mr. Krall, whose cold, stony composure gave away nothing.

They had planned everything before she was even hired. When Kevin gave her a note card with a red mark on the back, she wouldn't input it into the computer, but instead would take that note card and run it through the shredder so there wouldn't be any trace of evidence. The notecard was for the new flat-screen TV hanging on their living room wall. Kevin had it all figured out. He'd place the blame on some delivery driver who had been stealing appliances from the warehouse.

She gulped, cleared her throat, and said, "Yes, of course."

"All the Siralop Appliances family members must trust one another. Family members don't steal from the family. We aren't like those dysfunctional families you see on the T.V. talk shows. Almost everyone who works for me is a relation of sorts. The only two non-family members here are you and Mister VanZant."

This was the first time she had heard anything about that. It did make sense, since everyone else at Siralop Appliances had dark indigo eyes and very white teeth. "This I didn't know," was all she could think of as a reply.

"Well, it's true. We had a recent incident in which one of the flat-screen televisions wasn't delivered. Mister VanZant tried to blame everything on Sid. But Sid is family, and Sid wouldn't steal. Sid is trustworthy. You see, he was raised in the bright lights of Polaris. Your Sun is too dull, too shadowy, and lies and deceit thrive in the darkness."

Polaris. Siralop. Siralop is Polaris spelled backwards, Roberta thought. *Your Sun— Did this guy think he was some kind of alien? I thought he was a little bit eccentric; now I know he's totally bonkers.*

Roberta cleared her throat. "There must be some kind of mistake or something. Kevin wouldn't steal a flat-screen T.V. He loves his job. I'm sure if he were here, he could explain everything. But he's on family leave right now because of his sick father."

Mr. Krall's indigo eyes seemed to darken. "Yes, I agree. If Mister VanZant was here, a lot of things would get straightened out."

"Do you want to talk when he returns on Monday?"

"Yes, that would be a good idea. But before you leave, could you do me a favor and open the bottom drawer of that filing cabinet—the one to your left—and give me the only item inside?"

"Sure," Roberta said.

He just wants to check out my ass, she thought. Kevin would have to come up with a new plan or else they would both be fired, get arrested, and end up in jail.

Roberta slowly bent over, imagining Mr. VanZant's expression, how his eyes would be focused on her taut ass. When she slid open the file drawer, she didn't see a file. She pulled the drawer out a little more, and hot bile rose in her throat.

Inside was Kevin's head, his vacant eyes boring into her own.

"In *your* Bible," Mr. Krall said, "it says an 'eye for an eye'—and in some Middle Eastern countries, they'll cut off your hands for stealing. But since Mister VanZant was the head of this criminal operation, I took it upon myself to just cut off his head."

Roberta knew she had to run, but before she could even take the first step toward the door and freedom, Mr. Krall leaped up and over his desk like some kind of huge corporate toad, landing right in front of her. He grabbed her hand and upper arm, pulled her toward him.

"Where do you think you're going?" he hissed.

"Please let me go!" Roberta pleaded.

"As you wish," Mr. Krall said, letting go of her.

"Thank you," she said breathlessly, her eyes closed. She tried to rub away the growing pain in her arm.

With one smooth motion, Mr. Krall slammed her against the wall and ripped her blouse open, the black buttons scattering across the office floor.

"Oh my God, you're going to rape me—" Roberta cried.

Pinning Roberta to the wall, he yanked off her bra and savagely bit into her right breast, blood squirting into his open mouth.

At that moment, Charlene Maltin entered the office.

"Thank God, Charlene, Mister Krall has gone insane—" Roberta reached out to Charlene, who knocked her hand way. The secretary pressed against Roberta, nuzzling her other breast before tearing at it to get to the sweet, sweet blood.

The metallic scent of Roberta's blood drifted down the hall to the office of Daniel Levy, the accountant, where he and his son, Sid, the deliveryman, were talking about their weekend plans. Visibly flushed, they both hurried to Mr. Krall's office, where each lifted one of Roberta's wrists and began to gnaw away at her soft, supple flesh.

Just coming in from dumping the last of the office shredders into the recycling bin, Jerry Leonard, the janitor, sniffed, then sniffed again. "Happy Hour at the office! Far out!" Within moments, he was between Roberta's legs, blissfully lapping at the blood trickling down her body.

Mr. Krall politely belched, then wiped the remaining blood from his face with a handkerchief. Charlene finished licking the blood from her lips, then popped a fresh cube of strawberry bubble gum into her mouth and started chewing.

Reaching behind one of the filing cabinets, Mr. Krall pulled out and handed Charlene a "Help Wanted" sign. "Please be so kind as to hang this out front before you leave, Charlene," he said. "We need some new blood in the office."

HUNTER'S MOON

She ran naked through the woods. Huge trees occasionally blocked her path, but she simply circled around them. Running... Running... Running...

But to where? The only thing she knew for certain was that she was alone in a dark, strange forest. Not a good place to be.

She kept running.

The wet grass and mulch chilled her feet. She could see her breath in the air. Her heart was burning inside her chest, beating against her ribs with such force she thought it would burst through at any moment. But she did not dare stop running.

She heard a noise—a wheeled metal vehicle rushing down the road. She hit the ground, lying low. The lights of the vehicle came closer, glaring.

She pressed her body into the earth. Her lips brushed against rough dirt. What sort of creatures, she wondered, coiled and writhed inside the alien machine? She felt cornered, trapped. This was surely the end.

The vehicle hurried by and kept on moving.

She was safe—for the moment. Still cautious, she stood slowly and watched as the lights on the back of the metal machine faded into the night.

Just a few hours before, she had been the commander of a starship, passing through the planetary system of a star known to her people as Ka. Rogue energy waves from a passing comet had knocked out the ship's navigational computer, necessitating an emergency landing on Ka's third planet.

Out of control, the starship had swirled into the rocks at the bottom of a deep lake. Her two crewmates, stationed in the front of the ship's top deck, were killed in the crash. Her workstation in the back of the lower deck had sustained less damage, and so her life was spared. She managed to escape the submerged ship, opening a hatch to a flood of cold water.

She was covered in mud when she finally made it to the lake's shore. Her work garments were torn, wet, and filthy. She removed them and threw them back into the water.

She looked around. Dark woods lay ahead of her, so she did the only thing left to do: She ran.

Standing on a hillside, she stared up at the low orange moon. It was so strange to only see one. On her world, there were three moons—one blue, one gray, and one dusky red—in the night sky. Sometimes the red moon would take on a bright orange glow, and her people would call that the Hunter's Moon, since it gave the night creatures light to pursue their prey.

This planet also had a Hunter's Moon.

Even though she was feverish from running, the night's cool air chilled her skin. Her body felt strange—hot on the inside, cold on the outside.

As if she had wished it to be so, she suddenly spotted a dwelling down in a nearby clearing. The same vehicle she'd seen earlier was stationed next to the dwelling. Her instincts told her to run in the opposite direction, to rush as far away as she could. But still, she needed to find shelter. Her only choice was to explore whatever options the dwelling might provide.

She crept up to the dwelling, peered through the side window, and saw a male humanoid. He was tall, dark-haired, and wore tight garments that accentuated his body's firm musculature. She felt another kind of heat rushing down to her groin.

She sniffed and licked her lips. He was drinking a beverage from a glass container as he sat in front of a small, flaming portal. She could hear the crackling of the fire, smell the aromatic smoke, and taste the smooth, spicy drink inside his mouth.

One part of her wanted to rip his flesh from his body; another part wanted to rut like a wild beast. She kept watching the humanoid, trying to control her impulses. Only a few hours earlier, she had been the commander of a spaceship. Who was she now?

In the morning, she awoke covered in blood.

Her senses on alert, she saw blood spattered all over the wooden walls and floors of the dwelling. Where was the male humanoid? She looked down to discover she was lying on what remained of him, his once-soft garments now stiff with dried blood.

She ran her tongue around her mouth. It tasted foul, coppery. She spat out gore. Her groin was slick with strange seeds—and her mind was a blank. How could she not remember killing or mating with the humanoid? Apparently, she had done both.

There was something wrong with her body's chemistry. Something more than simply the crash-landing had *changed* her, albeit briefly. The existence of a wheeled vehicle, as well as the various small machines she could see within the dwelling, indicated that this was a technology-based world inhabited by a humanoid race—and orbited by just one moon. It had to be that single moon in the sky that was messing with her bio-systems. She'd never had amnesia after eating or fornicating before. And she'd certainly never *devoured* a lover before.

She looked around the dwelling. It was a gruesome mess. But still, it held possibilities. She could stay here until she met up with another starship. Her people would come for her, eventually.

She looked down at what was left of the humanoid. A pity. He had been rather attractive. Once.

Until she had this new world figured out, she had better be careful. It wouldn't work for her to draw undue attention—especially since this planet's technology might have spotted her starship. Perhaps they would be able to locate her starship...and her. Maybe the aliens were already coming for her. She would be hunted, detained—and worse.

The dwelling was already starting to smell of decay, so she took the remaining chunks of the humanoid and hid them out in the forest. She found a stream and washed the blood from her body. It felt good to be clean again.

Later, she examined every machine, every object in the dwelling for hours, hoping to learn more about this strange world.

Eventually, she fell asleep.

When she awoke, she felt—strange. But it wasn't a bad feeling. She looked down and saw that her body was now covered in gray fur. Again, strange. And yet, somehow, it felt very *right*.

She no longer had hands, but she managed to open the door of the dwelling with her jaws and paws. The moon was full in the night sky. The Hunter's Moon.

She heard a resonant howl. Turning swiftly, she saw a pack of other gray, furry night creatures—and they weren't in attack mode. They happily waggled the red tongues that lolled from their long, dark muzzles.

She was being welcomed.

As the night creatures started running through the forest and into the night, she joined them.

For an odd moment, she worried about whether her people would ever be able to find her. But then a strange new part of her mind assured her that everything was fine, fine, fine.

She was with her people *now*.

MOVING TO MARS — NO FORWARDING ADDRESS

It had all been so sudden... Who knew their name would come up in the first lotto?

With only a week to prepare for the launch from Upham, New Mexico, at the Southwestern Regional Spaceport, Lenore Peterson was afraid she'd forget something important. She couldn't help but chuckle at the irony of the spaceport being just east of the town of Truth or Consequences. The question was still implied to her. Yes, would she pick truth or consequences? Like truth or dare, it possessed a certain ominous potential.

Knowing the truth, then acting on it, was certainly opening one-self up to consequences. Too many people didn't want to know the truth. They'd rather believe the rhetoric that things were going to be just fine here on Earth. They wouldn't, not for a long time. Now, her future was as bright as the stars in the southwestern skies.

"Just pack the essentials," the facilitators had urged. *But how does one define those?* she mused, glancing over at the stack of boxes prepared for donation. She was going to change her tactics now: Just pack a few things and not worry about the other stuff. Some new families would move into their house, sleep in their beds, use their stuff... It felt very strange and exciting leaving her earthly goods behind.

They were allowed two bins each, and those would be transported in a different ship. Just one carry-on each for the trip to Mars. That's all they would need. Everything else would be provided for them. Two things came to mind that she wanted to pack: A box of chocolate candy and *The Wizard of Oz* by L. Frank Baum. It seemed like she had read the book a million times, back when she was around her daughter's age now. Like Dorothy, she was heading for a faraway land. She wouldn't be in Kansas—or, in this case, Las Cruces—anymore.

She packed some of the children's stuff with her belongings. Their books and art supplies, mainly, as they'd have new computer consoles when they arrived. The program facilitators promised never-before-seen game cartridges for the kids.

There was barely time to inform her mother, her ex, the school, and her soon-to-be-former employer. "Moving to Mars—yes, that's right... We're moving to Mars!" Lenore twirled around the room, the sound of her own laughter an incredible boon.

She couldn't remember the last time she'd laughed for joy, or what the occasion for that laugh had been, but this—*this* was certainly the occasion for it.

The house started shaking, and Lenore steadied herself against the kitchen counter. Another asteroid, most likely. There had been a broadcast earlier that morning about them. The newest wave of these would probably burn up when entering the atmosphere, but from the feel of it, at least one had made it through.

Probably in San Diego or Tijuana. It was amazing how the shocks could resonate all the way to Las Cruces. Thankfully, the tremors stopped. Lenore paused, then returned to her mental list of things to do.

The Mars Relocation Program provided change-of-address forms, but she didn't know what to write down as a forwarding address. There weren't addresses like on Earth—at least not yet. Most of the habitats were named after physicists and propulsion experts, founders, and sponsors. There was The Branson, named after a man who had invested in the project years ago, way back in 2010 or thereabouts.

She'd seen the diagrams. They reminded her of those old hippy communes, with geodesic domes grouped like Native American teepees.

Lenore somehow felt that the images had been altered, but she didn't care. They were moving to Mars! The kids would be so excited when they came home from school. It would be an adventure, and they sure could use some excitement in their lives, not to mention a positive change.

Karen, who had just turned eleven, would probably love the idea of being home-schooled by her mom, but Zach, who was nearly fourteen, would probably rather be out exploring. They would adjust. Kids, after all, are usually more resilient than their parents...given time.

Now, they had that time to adjust to their current life transitions: the divorce, their father's remarriage, the new baby, the adjoining neighborhoods ravaged by floods.

Yes, she'd have time to adjust to a new career, a new home, a new view outside her bedroom window. Change, as the meta-physicists said, was the only constant in the universe. Maybe she'd even start dating, what with the promise of all those single men on Mars—better than what Alaska had offered before the caps melted.

Moving to Mars was a proactive decision—yes! She was acting, in control of her—and her children's—lives. With a little help from the Mars Relocation Program...

What Lenore was really looking forward to was the peace and quiet. No more loud neighbors arguing or partying like it was the end of the world—which, in a way, it was. No more barking dogs or yowling cats...or their droppings. No more trash collection at the crack of dawn on Thursdays or having to drag the canisters back up the steep walkway to her driveway. No more dealing with bus pick-ups and drop-offs. No more endless hours of kids' homework.

Yes, she could kiss her old routines good-bye!

Then there was the luxury of climate-controlled insulated housing! It would be so cozy in the winter, too. Lenore fantasized while she tossed her favorite sweatsuit into the cargo case, followed by a small bag of sunscreen and cosmetics, a roll of deluxe condoms—just in case!

Yes, she would be happier on Mars, as would her kids. Their dad, his new wife, and their baby would even be happier without the awkward strain of a melded family.

Every one of the new waves of colonists—or perhaps *refugees* was the better word—would be happier.

And all thanks to the Mars Relocation Program. She shuddered at the thought of not being chosen at all, of not taking the risk to put herself and the kids up for the lotto. She quickly erased the thought from her mind. It was too depressing to think about in her current fiesta mood.

Lenore turned on the satellite TV to see if there was any coverage of the recent asteroid storm. All she got was static, so she turned it off, busied herself with packing. The kids wouldn't be home from their dad's place for a few hours still, and she could hardly wait to tell them the news.

It was hard to imagine that some people—even her neighbors, the McInernys across the street—never even entered the lotto. "What's the use?" Sheila had said, already accepting the inevitable. "Hal and I don't have kids. They want people with kids."

That was the first Lenore had heard of this. Only people with kids? Maybe Sheila knew something she didn't? Where was it that Hal worked again? She couldn't remember, even though she recalled Sheila mentioning it more than once, out of earshot of her husband— something to do with computers.

She would miss her daily visits with Sheila, usually over coffee and whatever else was available since the food rationing had begun. Thank the four corners she and the kids wouldn't have to deal with rations once they landed on Mars!

They were moving, moving to *Mars!* It still hadn't quite sunk in; probably wouldn't feel real until they were en route. The kids probably wouldn't sleep a wink tonight.

Lenore felt a little twinge. Was she doing the right thing? Maybe it was just global revision rather than global catastrophe... Her mind awhirl with floating cities on man-made landmasses, she tossed a pile of tank tops into a donation box marked "Women's Clothing: Summer."

The artificial landmasses were probably a thing of the future, but natural ones kept popping up all over the planet—especially just off the coast. The ocean was giving up its land in acres of encrusted mounds.

She couldn't help but wonder how many people made it into the first lotto—or the next. Would she know any of them? Was it a real lotto, or were they screening ahead of time? "People with kids," Sheila had said. "Just people with kids."

It made sense, though. Children were the future—always have been and always will be. They adapted to change quicker and generally learned faster than adults. They didn't have so much to unlearn, either.

But why her? She'd produced healthy children, was still healthy herself, and could probably have had more kids if the situation presented itself. Being a linguist would be useful, as Mars would be populated with people from all over Earth. Being a thirty-year-old divorced woman with two kids might have been her ticket to Mars! Though she kept wondering: Was there something else? Something they weren't being told.

Lenore wedged several of Karen's favorite books in with her clothes, making sure there was still enough room for the *Harry Potter* set she was rereading for the fifth or sixth time. Time! The days would be longer on Mars, 24.7 hours instead of 24. Instead of 365 days in a year, on Mars there would be 687, more than double an Earth year. So many more things could be done in one year on Mars than on Earth; the possibilities seemed endless, almost magical. If ever there was a time and a place needing magic, this was surely it.

Besides, life on Mars might just be magical—though the promotional materials probably had been edited by PR people. She remembered the decrypted images that had followed her relocation packet. Geodesic domes grouped together like teepees, or an old hippie commune, by a lovely stream...the moon's reflection, rippling... It was quite lovely. Then there were those pictures of the Martians welcoming them, their red arms outstretched against a backdrop of golden pyramids. Sun City, it was called, albeit loosely translated into English from their native tongue.

She remembered seeing one image that looked really retouched. It was a picture of one of their Mayan altars. Somehow, it looked too...clean. Plus, the native words on the side of the altar had been changed. She knew the language, and the words in the picture were simply meaningless gibberish. Well, that's what PR people do! They make everything look nice and clean and silly!

It was nice of those Mayans to leave a forwarding address, she thought. Nicer still that she was able to translate their language, so she would have a better idea than most of what to expect once they arrived. Of course, the task of translation always has its share of difficulties, but her background in linguistics would certainly help her out.

Amazing how those Mayans had managed to find their way to Mars—without rocket ships, even! Mayans... Weren't those the folks who used to sacrifice hearts? She tried to remember what she knew about them. They used to sacrifice the hearts of children to some god named Tláloc—but why? She seemed to recall they had a pretty good reason. Of course, all that was many, many *centuries* ago! Surely, the Mayans didn't do *that* anymore.

The house started shaking again. She started to run across the room so she could crawl under her desk for protection. Then it stopped—but not before her old, framed wedding photo fell off the wall. She didn't even bother to clean it up.

Probably another asteroid—had to be closer this time. As close as Santa Fe, or a little further away, like Reno? This was one of the things she wasn't going to miss on Mars.

Oh, Mars would be lovely this time of year—or so the brochure said. This would be the rainy season, when light, lovely showers made exotic flowers spring up. Rain on Mars! Apparently, the Mayans had figured out how to make that happen. Probably part of their advanced native super-science.

Rain, that was it! The Mayans used to sacrifice the hearts of children to make it *rain.*

She stopped packing for a minute. A funny thought had entered her head, only to flutter back out like a frightened moth.

She glanced at the clock on the wall. The kids would be home soon, so there wasn't much time left! She hurried up the packing. Yes, this would be an adventure the whole family could enjoy—especially the children!

She often thought about moving to a new location, a new place—but she'd never thought it would be Mars!

Mars, the red planet!

EXTRA CREDIT

Regina Mander hated night school. She yawned, then yawned again, wishing she had chosen the Saturday morning class instead. There were just too many distractions at the evening course: Professor Diaz strolling up and down the aisles; Todd Coombes clicking and unclicking his ballpoint pen; Jeffrey Blackwell drawing dirty sketches in his notebook; Ellie Lloyd's cell phone constantly going off.

To make matters worse, Regina's stomach was growling—she'd had a cheeseburger and chili fries for lunch, but that was hours ago, and the hunger came crawling back inside her tummy with a vengeance.

Then there was the biggest distraction of all: Tasha Prine with her shiny black hair slicked back with fragrant oil, the Japanese lettering tattooed up and down her arms, her ears filled with stainless steel studs and rings, her pierced nose, her uniform of black turtleneck, greasy black leather jacket, sleek torn blue jeans, and lizard skin boots.

"It's not a fashion statement," Tasha said when she noticed Regina was looking at her. "I get cold so easily," she said with her lisp of a voice, which made her sound like a little girl trapped in the body of a woman.

The class seemed to bore Tasha, and yet she was there every night. Before class was over, she'd slip out the back and disappear before Regina ever got a chance to see where she was going, curious as to what she was up to for some strange reason.

Regina had noticed her the first night of class, how she seemed older, didn't really seem to fit in with the class. She guessed Tasha's age to be in her late twenties, maybe even her early thirties. The guys checked her out but rarely approached her. Professor Diaz seemed a bit obsessed with her, the way his eyes would always focus on her with longing and just a hint of fear, too.

For Regina, it was those obsidian eyes and how she just knew Tasha saw into that place where she hid her darkest fantasies. She shuddered just thinking about the things she wished Tasha would do to her, what she would, with a bit of shy coaxing, do for Tasha.

Todd turned around to ask Regina something, but she didn't want to talk to him. Not since the time he'd given her a ride home and had slid his hand up her thigh all the while he was driving. Not since he'd patted her on the ass as she climbed out of his convertible. Todd was so uncouth with how he would bump into her in the hall-way—copping a quick feel of her breasts. He had no class. No class at all.

"I told you to leave me alone," she hissed, and Professor Diaz glared at them both.

"It's cool," Todd quickly recoiled. When the professor walked in the other direction, he uttered "bitch" under his breath.

Professor Diaz walked up and down the aisles with his hands held behind his back. Occasionally, he would lean over a student's shoulder, watch their hands moving pen across paper. He would nod occasionally, mumble something, and then move on. He rarely looked at what Tasha was writing, though, which underlined Regina's suspicions that there was something going on with these two. She sighed wistfully, realizing she probably didn't have a chance with Tasha if she was seeing the teacher. If Tasha were indeed the teacher's pet, she wouldn't have a chance at all.

Regina had to admit she came to class to see Tasha, even though they never spoke more than a few words at each class meeting. Then again, didn't they always exchange some kind of meaningful gaze, even though Regina wasn't sure of the meaning? She often felt Tasha was in her mind; it was just a touch, almost a caress of a thought, as if she were quietly entering a room to check on a sleeping baby, then pausing for a moment to enjoy the exquisite beauty of their innocence.

Regina imagined Tasha wandering the streets of downtown San Diego, stopping at this and that cafe, stirring her espresso while reading a book or writing. Perhaps she was an insomniac—or maybe she preferred the moon to sunlight. Even though she was beautiful to Regina, there were often dark circles under Tasha's eyes. Her black hair lacked any shine, and her skin seemed too pale, as if she hadn't slept or eaten in days. *Maybe the teacher is keeping her up late at night with extracurricular activities*, she thought.

After class this time, though, Tasha hovered around Professor Diaz, and then they left together. Regina followed them to Cafe del Noche, that trendy new place where everyone seemed anorexic and anemic and wore slinky black clothes, smoked clove cigarettes, and talked about the latest art exhibit. She knew she didn't quite fit in, but she walked in anyway, waited in line. Sometimes, it was good to be around people, even if they appeared to be hipper than you were.

Regina ordered a cherry mocha and found a table in the corner where she could watch them from a safe distance. They sat outside under the stars. Professor Diaz slowly sipped his espresso, while Tasha lazily stirred a spoon around in hers, toying with the lemon peel.

Tasha turned around and looked through the window, right into Regina's eyes. She smiled knowingly, reassuringly, and then returned her gaze to Professor Diaz, who seemed so at ease with her outside class. After an hour or so, the two left the cafe, arm-in-arm, Tasha's laughter reaching above Professor Diaz's low, resonant voice.

Regina tried to imagine them together—Tasha's bedroom must be permeated with Attar of Roses. The scent of burning incense, sandalwood, no—Nag Champa—would fill the air, along with a hint of something else. Something musky. Something metallic. Something unusual—both sensual and scary at the same time.

Attar of Roses was Tasha's favorite scent. During class, Regina always noticed when Tasha reached into her voluminous bag for the antique glass and silver atomizer covered with tiny pewter roses. She would tilt her head back, close her eyes, and spray the perfume in a trail down her long, lovely neck. The room would blossom with the scent of her long after she was gone. And in the middle of the night, Regina would swear she smelled the scent in her own bedroom, when she was curled alone beneath heavy blankets and comforters.

The next night at class they had a substitute teacher; it seemed Professor Diaz was sick or something.

"I'm sure he'll be back next week," the sub said. "My name is Donald Waterman. You can call me Don if you like."

Regina looked around the room at her fellow students. Tasha was also absent, which was strange, as she'd never missed a class before. They must be all wrapped up in each other in front of a burning fireplace, Regina mused, seething with jealousy.

Class ended early that night, and the substitute shrugged off their concerns. "Just follow the syllabus," Don instructed.

At the next class meeting, they had the same sub, Don—bald and fat and wearing a cheap suit. "Still no sign of Professor Diaz," he said. Regina was curious. Had they run off together? Maybe they were in an accident or something. Maybe Professor Diaz was married, and his wife killed both for having an affair. Even though there hadn't been anything on the news, it was just too coincidental.

Then Tasha strolled through the door. Regina's relieved smile was not lost on Tasha.

Don-the-Sub, let them out early again. As her classmates milled out of the room, Regina took her time reorganizing the books and papers in her backpack. The scent of roses wafted around her. She felt the firm pressure of a hand.

"Regina, want to have a coffee with me?"

"Sure."

"Cafe del Noche?"

"That sounds awesome." Regina almost kicked herself for saying, "awesome," as she was sure Tasha would think of her as a teenager, which she was, technically, for another month before she officially entered the "twenty-something" years.

Regina and Tasha walked away from campus, then down the sparsely lit side streets that lead to Cafe del Noche. Tasha insisted on treating and ordered a cherry mocha for Regina and an espresso for herself—paying with a large bill and telling the barista to keep the change.

While Regina chattered nervously about what had happened in class the last time, and how the band Meat Wagon was going to play on campus the next week, Tasha listened patiently, stirring, but never drinking, her now-cold espresso.

Tentatively, Tasha rested a hand on Regina's. Regina didn't move. She couldn't breathe as she looked directly into Tasha's eyes and offered a weak smile. Tasha grasped her hand, explored each finger, pressing here and there, slowly circling the palm with a long purple nail. Regina shivered.

"Follow me," Tasha said.

Regina did as they walked outside the café. Between the café and a big brick building, Tasha took Regina's hands in her own again, then placed her lips to Regina's index finger, licking, then sucking it into her mouth. She did the same with the rest of Regina's fingers.

"Let's go to my place," Tasha said, almost breathless, still with the little girl's voice, but it was very sexy, too.

They walked down the street hand-in-hand, Tasha drawing Regina closer with each step. She ran her finger along the side of Regina's face and gave a suggestive smile.

After a few more blocks, they turned into a loft complex. *How fitting*, Regina thought.

It was dark inside, so dark that Regina couldn't see a thing. After a while, her eyes adjusted, and she watched as Tasha struck a match, then lit a group of candles.

"Would you like something to drink? Some music, perhaps?"

"Water would be nice."

"I'm sorry; I am all out of bottled water. I do have some wine."

"I'm not quite old enough for wine," Regina said, then wished she hadn't, as it made her feel like a little girl.

"No, I.D.s required here," Tasha said with that provocative smile. "It's a good wine, a Coppola, from the movie director's vineyard."

Tasha returned with a bottle of red wine. "Sorry, all my cups are dirty."

Regina opened it slowly, then tilted the bottle back, drinking a little of the wine before setting it on the table. She noticed how intently Tasha watched her drink, how her eyes traveled from her hands to her mouth, down her neck, then rested on her shoulders.

Tasha slinked across the room toward Regina, who sighed as the other woman gently stroked her cheek. "Let's take off this shirt," she murmured. Then, Tasha trailed one of her long purple nails across her jaw, underneath her neck, where she rested her fingers, felt the vein throbbing against her fingertips. With her other hand, she slowly ran it down from her shoulder to her breast; she circled her nipple with a thumb, then the other, pinching them occasionally, smiling when Regina moaned and pressed against her.

"So soft, so soft," Tasha murmured as she pulled off her own shirt to feel skin against skin. Tasha wound her hand around and around Regina's long red hair, before clamping her mouth around Regina's.

Their lips locked with a fierce passion; Tasha slid her tongue into Regina's mouth.

"Oh, Gina," Tasha softly moaned.

"No, it's Regina."

"Oh, Gina," Tasha softly kissed again.

Regina just let it slide because she was caught up in the passion.

After releasing her from the kiss, she laughed delightedly and announced, "I'm going to tie you up."

She led Regina to the futon, skillfully bound her arms over her head, looping the cord through the boards, tying first one ankle, then the other to the slats at the end.

Kneeling before her, Tasha unzipped her jeans and tugged them and her thin, pink silk panties down until she could slip her fingers, then her hand, between swollen folds of skin, between the wispy red curls of her opening.

"Ooh, so wet, my love," she said between long kisses.

Regina spasmed, thrashed around on the bed to the sound of Tasha's resonant chuckle.

"You are going to be fun to play with. I knew I was right about you."

Tasha pressed Regina's thighs further apart, revealing the fullness of her blood-engorged sex.

"So lovely," she crooned, trailing her fingers up along the insides of her thighs, extending her tongue to lap, then suckled the moisture, taking the plump mound into her mouth as Regina tugged against the restraints.

"Oh—that was so good, Tasha," she sighed, then was startled from her erotic reverie by the touch of warmer, more gentle hands.

"Who's that?" She opened her eyes, strained to lift her head from the futon to see.

"Cover her eyes, darling. I don't want to spoil our little surprise."

"Professor Diaz? Is that you?"

"And cover her mouth, too," he added, smiling wickedly at Tasha.

"Javier, darling, doesn't Regina need an extra credit assignment or two?"

"Yes, something like that," he chuckled.

They laughed, and Regina would have joined in if she could, but something told her she must be frightened, the fun and games were over, and the real purpose of her being there was fast approaching.

She'd forgotten all about the bliss earlier in the evening as one on each side, they untied her legs, then bent and pressed her knees against her chest. Regina shivered uncontrollably as she felt their chill breath against her skin. Fingers lightly traced the path of a desired vein before their fangs penetrated her flesh. Moans and screams continued through the night.

FOR BETTER AND FOR WORSE

The brick house with an enormous chimney and too many hedges in the front yard remained quiet during the daylight hours. But as the sun set, it was a different story. Shades were pulled up. Lights in various rooms were turned on, and so was the oversized television.

"Honey... Will you come in here, please?" Sam Nelson asked, concerned.

His wife, Myra, padded into the bathroom.

"Yes, dear?" She lingered in the doorway while Sam picked at something on his chin.

"The super glue isn't working. Look!" Sam held up a long strip of skin.

"Oh dear—you're right. Absolutely right. Hold on. I'll be right back in a moment."

While waiting for his wife to return, Sam resisted the impulse to keep picking at the loose skin on his face. It was beginning to bubble up along his neck, too. He lifted his fingers to his frayed nostrils, sniffed—then started coughing at the stench.

"For better and for worse," his wife, Myra, had said on their wedding day. Well, if there ever was a worse, this was certainly it. Who knew that the recessive gene would come out after puberty!

Who knew?

If only his parents were still alive. They would know what to do.

He set the toilet lid down gently. It wouldn't do to get all upset. Myra would know what to do. She would have a solution. She always stayed calm and rational... It was one of the many reasons he'd married her.

But what if she wouldn't stay with him now that the family condition was getting worse? Kids were out of the question now that he clearly had the mutant gene. And it seemed to be getting worse every day. Pretty soon, all his skin would slough off to reveal this bizarre pinkness underneath.

Sam sniffed at his fingers again. Shuddered.

Myra returned with a scarf. Suddenly, he knew what he had to do but was just dreading it. He wrapped the scarf around his head, covering most of his disfigured face.

It had been an hour since Sam had left; he kept driving the SUV down the dark streets, looking for the right opportunity to present itself. Usually, it was some junkie wandering alone; sometimes, it was a homeless person or a hooker looking for a trick.

He couldn't believe his luck. He saw a Mustang convertible pulled over to the side of the road; a young blonde co-ed was standing next to her car with the hood open. Sam stopped his SUV and walked over to the young girl. "What seems to be the problem?" he asked.

"I don't know," she said. "The car just died."

Sam joined her at the front of the car. He looked down at the engine. As she cast her gaze downward, he struck.

Flinging off the scarf, he savagely bit the back of her neck. Blood gushed over the engine block, grill, and bumper, dripping from the fender. He wrapped the scarf tightly around her mouth to muffle her scream. With one swift move, he broke her neck and gnawed on her tender flesh.

Sam returned home, his clothes covered in blood. He'd burn them in the fireplace tomorrow night. He took a long, hot shower, dried off, and climbed into bed with the sleeping Myra. "For better and for worse." It was better now.

RHIANNON

The eighth-grade literature class bored Josh Monday. The whole eighth grade bored him. He was counting down the days until he would enter high school, hoping it would have more to offer. He needed a change. Anything would be better than middle school.

His teacher, Mrs. Stone, was droning on and on about *The Red Badge of Courage* and what a great book it was.

Hell, Josh thought, *Stephen Crane didn't even fight in the Civil War.* He was a journalist, and anybody could write a war book if they interviewed enough people about it. The book should have been called *The Red Book of Correspondences.*

Josh had read the book the night before. With one ear and a headphone hidden under his locks of dark hair, he was listening to Metallica's Black Album, which was called, simply, *Metallica.* He had burned the CD from his dad and was listening to the song, "Sad, But True." The other ear didn't have the headphones on just in case Mrs. Stone asked him a question during class.

Josh wasn't worried about missing the boring lecture because he was taping it with his pocket cassette player. During study hall, he would re-listen to it and write down any facts that might be on a test; for the rest, he would just fast-forward. There wasn't much to do during study hall anyway—unless his friend, Skylar Calvin, would sneak in an issue of *Playboy* that he stole from his older brother, Scott.

Josh had discovered he liked women with big breasts, but there weren't many of those around in the eighth grade, except for Veronica O'Keeffe, who was very chesty, but she was dating the school's quarterback, and, of course, Mrs. Stone, who was nicknamed "Mrs. Brickhouse" after an old Commodores song.

There were only about fifteen minutes left in class, then study hall time, maybe looking-at-glossy-photos-of-large-breasts time if Skylar brought the new issue. Something caught the corner of his eye, a movement to the side of him. He turned around and saw a girl sitting behind Skylar's chair.

That's odd, Josh thought. *That seat's been empty all semester.*

Josh slowly turned his head to get a better look at the girl. She had long strawberry-blonde hair that covered most of the left side of her face, and she was wearing a light-gray dress.

That's odd, too, Josh thought. *Nobody wears dresses these days. It's either baggy jeans, jeans with holes in them, miniskirts, or leggings.*

He looked into the eye on the right side of her face that wasn't buried in her hair. It was round and sad and gazing down toward the ground. He glanced at the spotted tile floor and saw nothing of interest, so Josh returned to study her pouty red lips. They didn't look like they'd formed a smile for a long time.

He didn't know why, but he thought—no, he *knew*—she was pretty when she smiled. It was like he'd seen her somewhere before, light shining through that silky strawberry-blonde hair...

At that moment, the bell rang. Josh reached down to grab his book bag, wanting to sneak one last look at this mysterious new girl—but she was gone.

Josh walked the six blocks home, hoping his mother was out running errands, as she usually did on Friday. He wanted to be alone, listen to the Metallica CD with two ears instead of one, and maybe sneak a peek at one of his old *Playboys*. If he was lucky, he could yank himself good before his mom got home.

The sky started to darken as Josh rounded the corner to his house. A few raindrops spattered on his head. *That's weird,* he thought. *Whoever heard of it raining in May in Camarillo, California?*

The spatters turned into a drizzle, and the drizzle, a torrent, as Josh ran the half-block or so home. He fumbled for the key in his front pocket, unlocked the door, and cursed as the wind blew sideways, knocking his binder out of his hands, papers scattering everywhere.

"Shit! Shit-shit-shit!" Josh muttered, pushing the door open, then crouching down to collect the soggy papers. As he stood up, just out of the corner of an eye, he saw *her* again. The girl with sad brown eyes. Her hair still hung over one side of her face, strangely unmoved by the wind. Her gray dress, which he realized she filled out quite nicely, was curiously dry.

"Hey," Josh said. "I saw you in lit class today. I'm Josh Monday." He stuck out his hand, realized it was wet, and wiped it on his jeans. The girl just looked at him like he was strange for offering his hand in the first place. He stuck both his hands in his pockets.

"And you are...?"

She studied him a while longer, bit, then sucked on her lower lip. "Kathleen Rhiannon McBride—but I prefer being called Rhiannon rather than Kathleen or Katie like my mum calls me." And then she curtsied a bit. *An old-fashioned girl,* Josh thought. *And not from around here.* She had to be a foreign exchange student or something.

"Wanna come in? Get out of the rain?" Josh turned toward the foyer, listened for a bit, and realized that the two of them were alone. Exquisitely alone. He would hate it if his mother watched these awkward attempts at romance. There would be no end of teasing if that happened.

When Josh turned around, Rhiannon was gone.

Shortly after six, Josh's mom arrived home. She brought some take-out Chinese for dinner but didn't eat any of the sesame chicken herself because she was going on a date with Steve from accounting. She took a quick shower, changed her clothes, and told him to do his homework and not to stay up late again.

For the rest of the night, Josh listened to Metallica's *S&M* CD. His dad had given it to him for Christmas last year. He hadn't seen much of his dad since the divorce three years ago, when he had just packed up and moved to New Jersey. Now, there was an entire country between them.

Metallica's hardcore fans and critics panned the *S&M* disc, but Josh thought it rocked. It reminded him of the movie *King Kong vs. Godzilla,* with two musical titans rocking out. Just imagine the powerful orchestra—the San Francisco Symphony—and rock band Metallica playing together! His father even attended both concerts, which were recorded for the CD, at the Berkley Community Theater on April 21 and 22, 1999.

Josh was listening to the song "Where I May Roam," and it was blasting out of his bedroom speakers. The song made him picture the Grim Reaper sitting all melancholy by a silent brook, lost in thought.

Josh had been drawing most of the night. He had done several charcoal sketches of Rhiannon: one, a close-up of her face, the others of her sitting at the desk.

His dog, a chubby beagle named Lars after Metallica's drummer, Lars Ulrich, laid his head on the bed and whimpered.

"What's the matter, boy?" Josh asked. He listened. The house was quiet. He was used to the house being quiet after the divorce, though. Before the divorce, it was full of angry shouts and slammed doors. He had lived his entire life in this house.

When he looked up, he saw her again.

"Hello, Josh," she said softly.

"Rhiannon." He put down his drawing.

"They're quite lovely," she said, picking up the drawing of the close-up of her face. "Is this how I look? It's beautiful."

"You're beautiful," Josh said. "I've been thinking about you all night. I know it sounds corny, but we've met before, haven't we? There's just something familiar about you. It's like— No, never mind."

"Go on. It's like what?" Rhiannon handed him the drawing.

"I keep seeing you gazing down at me. There's light shining in your hair, and you're happy. You look happy, like you're in-love."

Josh put his hands in his pockets. He wanted to reach out to her, to touch her, but he resisted.

Rhiannon walked to the bedroom window and looked out. The rain was pouring down then, and thunder crashed nearby.

"Unfortunately, love—or life—isn't forever," she said so softly that he had to lean forward to hear her.

"What do you mean?" Josh said. He put the drawing down and turned around—but Rhiannon was gone once again.

The next morning, Josh had some cold cereal for breakfast. A knock-off of a brand-name cereal; his mom said they were just as good and half the price. She was getting ready to go to work—and it was Saturday. It seemed like she went in on Saturdays more and more these days. Sometimes, he thought it was just an excuse to get out of the house.

She looked tired—the kind of tired it would take several cups of coffee to even dent. It was probably those sleeping pills again. Josh remembered when she took them all the time after the divorce. She said it was because her schedule was all turned upside-down.

"How was your date with Steve?" Josh asked.

"It was nice," his mom said. "Thanks for asking."

"Mom," he asked, "what do you do when you like a girl but you're not sure if she likes you back?"

"Oh, honey." His mom hugged him. "What girl?"

"Kathleen Rhiannon McBride."

His mom, who'd been standing, collapsed in a chair, her face several shades lighter than usual. Even her hands were shaking.

"Do you know her? Is there something wrong with her or something?" Josh asked.

"She lived in this house before we moved in. The McBrides sold this house and went back to England or Ireland. I'm not sure where.

They sold it below market value. They wanted to get rid of it after their only daughter, Kathleen Rhiannon McBride, committed suicide."

"What? You can't be serious, Mom. I've seen her. She's far from dead, she's—"

"She's dead, sweetie. This girl you like must be playing some sort of sick prank on you."

"Why would she do that?" Josh shook his head, incredulous. This really took the prize. He went through his mind trying to think who would put her up to this—and why. He couldn't think of anyone who would be that much of a jerk.

Josh's mom reached out to take his hand in hers. "Josh, people do strange things. It's possible this girl is mentally disturbed. I assure you that the real Kathleen Rhiannon McBride died in this house, in her bedroom, fifteen years ago, just a few months before we moved in and you were born."

"When did she die, Mom? When?"

"I'm not sure of the exact date, but you were born on the second of July, so it would have been sometime during the first week of May."

"Mom, don't you get it? It's the first week of May now."

Her hands trembled around his, then clenched his tighter before letting go.

"It's just not possible. There's another explanation. Stay away from that girl!" she cried out, pushing off the table to stand up. "I need to get to work. There's a staff meeting."

Josh thought she looked like she was going to faint, hurl—or both. He knew the girl had to be who she claimed to be. It explained why she seemed to disappear into thin air, then reappear out of nowhere. But why him? Did she need his help? She must. He had seen her before. He knew he had.

Josh was still sitting at the breakfast table when he heard his mother close and lock the door. She'd left a twenty on the table for pizza or whatever. He folded it up, slipped it into his pocket, then waited for Rhiannon to visit him again. He knew she'd be there again—and soon.

He wanted it to be so. He waited and waited and waited and waited. Nothing happened. Rhiannon wasn't there. "To hell with it," Josh said, heading back to his bedroom.

He stuck Metallica's *The Black Album* compact disc and listened to the song "Enter Sandman" on full volume until the windows in his room were shaking from the vibrations of the loud drum and basslines.

He took off his T-shirt and started to unbutton his pajama bottoms—normally, he didn't wear such things to bed, but the night before he did, just in case she showed up in the middle of the night.

The music changed. It was no longer Metallica, but soft jazz. The song was a remake of Cyndi Lauper's "Time After Time" but sung by Erin Bode, whose voice was silky smooth and sounded a lot like Norah Jones, who his friend, Skylar, had the major hots for.

Rhiannon appeared from behind. "You listen to too much Metallica," she said. "And you don't have to stop getting undressed because of me. That's what I was hoping you'd be doing. Would you give me a hand and unzip the back of my dress?"

Josh tugged the zipper until it clicked on the last track. She slid the gray dress over her shoulders, then dropped it to the floor. Underneath, she had on a light blue bra and matching panties. She unfastened the brassiere, and it, too, fell to the floor.

Her breasts weren't big like the ladies in *Playboy,* but they were well-proportioned for her size. She unbuttoned his pajama bottoms and pulled down his jockey shorts. When she knelt before him and took him inside her mouth, he thought he'd died and gone to heaven. Like most forms of happiness, it was over before he knew it.

A few minutes later, Rhiannon had slipped back into her gray dress and was in the bathroom, crying.

"What's the matter? Did I do something wrong?" Josh asked.

"I always cry afterward. My father molested me for years, and doing it always gives me bad memories," she said, blowing her nose and throwing the tissue in the toilet.

Josh hugged her tightly.

Rhiannon opened the medicine cabinet and took out a bottle of his mother's sleeping pills. She opened the lid.

"Last night, you said you thought you knew me. You do. I've watched you since you were born, waiting for you to grow up so we can be together. I'm only visiting, but if you want to be with me, take a handful of these pills and we will be together..." She paused. "...forever."

Josh was confused. His head was spinning—too many thoughts were racing around his mind at the same time. He knew he loved her and wanted to be with her forever. He knew taking the pills would be wrong, but he swallowed them anyway.

He went back into his bedroom and turned down the music. Metallica's "Enter Sandman" was playing. He closed his eyes and thought of Rhiannon and knew he'd be joining her soon.

SOLO STORIES

THE WAY HOME
Terrie Leigh Relf

January 2012

It was a cold night. Dark fog poised in the distance like a jaguar ready to pounce. Sochi paced back-and-forth in her candle-lit apartment's kitchen, waiting for Adon to come back. They were leaving before dawn, if not sooner...unless that fog had other plans for them.

Sochi toyed with an amulet tied around her neck, amazed she still clung to the belief that this old piece of jewelry would be their salvation.

"Never take it off," her grandmother had said, placing it around Sochi's neck the day before she died. "It will show you the way home."

Home. She looked out at the night through her bedroom window, sighing. San Diego was her home. Even though she still couldn't imagine living anywhere else, the water was rising. So much of the planet had been drastically altered.

She hadn't listened to the radio at all today, and not because she wanted to conserve batteries. Late last night, the broadcast said the evacuation process was winding down. There was the usual government rhetoric about having everything under control; thousands of people had been rescued and were now safely ensconced in government and private-sector compounds. Not to panic; there would be another contingent of rescue vehicles in their area.

Sochi turned off the radio. There hadn't been any rescue groups for days—maybe over a week. Not a single Navy or Coast Guard vessel, not a single rescue helicopter patrol. She didn't want to think about those who had perished. She had to focus on her and Adon surviving.

But what kind of world would they now inhabit?

Yes, she was one of the lucky ones. Was it fate, karma, or just pure good fortune that Adon's large extended family had boats: fishing boats, houseboats—even a medium-sized yacht. No one this generous family knew would be abandoned. Even Adon had his own boat, a birthday gift from his uncle. He had named it *The Star Gazer*, after his mother's favorite flower, the Star Gazer lily.

Sochi pulled back the curtains, looked out at the inky night. The moon was nearly full and surrounded by a burnt-orange haze. What if her grandmother's tales were nothing more than bedtime stories, nothing more than an old woman's overactive imagination mixed with hope that her granddaughter would survive?

It was loco, Sochi thought. So loco that it just might be true.

The scientific community had scoffed at the Mayan End of Days, arguing that even if global anomalies occurred, they wouldn't create the chaos that now surrounded her, that now encompassed the entire planet.

But her ancestors knew. Her grandmother had known. And now the world knew.

It was loco, and now it had come to pass.

Sochi traced the misshapen figure on the amulet's back, seeing the winged man through her fingers and the touch of memory. Her grandmother had said, "It is Camazotz, the Bat God—and you will share the legacy of its blood. I wish I could return home with you, but my days will end before yours."

If someone had been eavesdropping, they would have believed her *abuelita* was going senile, perhaps suffering from dementia, or at the very least, experiencing a breakdown due to the irreversible deluge that was now reality.

But Sochi knew these stories. Her *abuelita* had shared them with her since she was a child, embellishing them from time-to-time, but the core story never changed. Just before she died, the stories had possessed an urgency, and in the hearing of them, an uncanny shudder of truth.

Her grandmother had claimed to being born on a distant planet, far beyond what the naked eye could see. It was named Aztlan and located past the Pleiades in the Alpha Centauri system.

Her grandmother an alien? It would explain so much, and yet, it was truly loco—as were the stories of the bat god's real purpose.

"How could I share blood with a bat?" Sochi had asked repeatedly, but all her grandmother did was repeat the litany.

But now Sochi believed—even hoped—it was true. As repulsive as sharing the blood of a bat sounded, it was probably just a figure of speech to pass down facts as legend. Together, she and Adon would unravel its meaning. They had to!

Adon had searched the internet for clues—even rummaged around the old library stacks—but there hadn't been many references to the Camazotzian. There were stories about bat gods and ritual blood sacrifices and other odds and ends, but nothing about drinking bat blood for transformation. Sochi had come across some Chinese medicine references to bat guano and teas, but that wasn't the same thing.

No, there was something different in the stories her grandmother told that deviated from these tales of ritual sacrifice. She focused on transformation, a melding of bat and man—or woman—as a means of returning home.

But where was home?

Her *abuelita* had said, "In the stars—there!" Then pointed through her bedroom window toward the Seven Sisters, the oldest of whom she could barely see. She had burned a sage stick then, as she did now, to purify herself, to dispel fear and an increasing sense of foreboding.

The necklace was old, but could it really be that old? Sochi grasped it in her hand, felt it begin to warm, to vibrate. Could this be an actual relic from Mayan times? An alien artifact? Had her grandmother—and her ancestors—really been from another planet?

"I'm not loco," she said aloud. "I'm not loco... I'm not loco... I'm not—"

"Sochi!" Adon called out as he slid the key into the door. She jumped off the bed to unfasten the deadbolt. Even though they were probably the last two people alive in the building, she still felt safer with the extra lock.

"Coming!" She opened the door and threw herself into Adon's arms as if it had been years, rather than hours, since they last saw each other.

"It's not as if I'm the last man on Earth," he chuckled, kissed her playfully, then more urgently. She pushed him away, giggled.

"I'm done packing." Sochi pointed to a beat-up old locker with rusty hinges and several duffle bags. "I used about a case of plastic zip-lock bags. It's hard to leave so many books behind, but I packed the important things."

He smirked at her, tousled her hair. "You're the most important thing—"

"Okay," she laughed. "Me and whatever this amulet is."

"I keep telling you it's a tracking device—or a communication device—like an alien G.P.S. unit!" Adon said, reaching for the charm dangling between her plump breasts. He lightly grazed the symbols that surrounded the pulsing stone.

"You see these symbols... At first glance, they look like the Mayan calendar, but they go counterclockwise, and aren't the same. Hey..." He laughed uneasily, said, "...maybe this amulet unravels time, and we'll go back to the way things were."

"You're freaking me out, Adon. Stop it!" She turned away from him and pleaded silently to her grandmother for a sign. How many of these amulets were there? She couldn't have the only one.

"Do you think there are others out there with these?"

"I've never seen one like it, but perhaps they're passed down within families like your grandmother did with you. A few museums have shards that resemble it, but not with these markings. Besides, they're made of clay and stone. This is neither. It's some sort of metal with quartz or something. Hematite? That's it. It's probably hematite. I heard they found hematite on the moon—or was it Mars? Those clay and stone ones are probably something the people created to pass down the knowledge and memory of the original."

"So now you're the expert!" Sochi punched him playfully.

"It's a feeling. You know, me, Soch, ever the optimist. I don't feel like this is the end of the world. It's not like the whole planet is submerged—"

"Yet," she whispered.

"And people thought Katrina was bad..." His voice trailed off as he pulled Sochi to him, stroked her blue-black hair that smelled of sage.

"Where do you think the survivors were taken?"

Adon shrugged. "Some place high off the ground. Colorado, probably. It's still above water last I heard. Some place far away from here."

"Do you ever regret not leaving with the others? I mean, this might be it. No going back," Sochi murmured.

"I just want this moment to last. Holding you right now like this, I almost feel like we've gone back in time. "

The candle began to sputter, then went out.

"Maybe that's a sign from my *abuelita* that it's time to go," Sochi murmured.

"Let me see that amulet again," Adon whispered. They leaned toward each other, forehead to forehead, to examine it more closely.

Adon wasn't sure if he was supposed to trace the pattern of etched and raised symbols clockwise or counterclockwise. He was sure they told a story—or provided some sort of instructions. In addition to the symbols for what appeared to be water, there were others for wind and fire—but not earth. The most curious, however, was an image that seemed to depict a subterranean vault or cave. Inside this space was some sort of craft. He always joked around with Sochi that she was descended from aliens, but what if she was? What if her *abuelita* hadn't been delusional at her death?

"What if this amulet's a key—the key—for this craft?"

"You watch too much science fiction T.V.," Sochi teased.

"But what if, Sochi? What if?"

"And what if it is? You still have the *cajones* to go with me?" she asked playfully, but inside, deep inside, she was afraid he wouldn't, that, at the last minute, he would leave her to join his family up the coast, and she would be alone.

Adon grinned. "You think you'll get rid of me that easily? I can't lie. I'm going to miss my family, but..."

"But?" Sochi turned away.

"But nothing. I will miss my family. I want to be with you—no matter what the consequences."

It was just after dawn; the fog had lifted enough to give them a modicum of visibility. While *The Star Gazer*'s motor warmed up, Adon read a note that Sochi's grandmother had scrawled as a final journal entry.

"I wish I could make this out. Something about a rocky outcropping by Point Loma?"

"The amulet and *Abuelita*'s journals will guide us. Do you remember that one series of paintings she did? The ones she wouldn't sell no matter what anyone offered her? Popi always said they were her best work, and mama... Mama was so unhinged that she insisted on hanging them in the living room."

"Yeah—there was that really strange one that looked like a womb to an alternate dimension or something."

"Yeah, with waves in the distance. Maybe they told another story. The story of leaving, of returning home."

"Maybe—but I'm worried there might be others waiting to board the spacecraft—if that's where this leads. Maybe it's just an underwater shelter—not a landing bay? Are we going to blast through the water or something? Tunnel underground? I'm not big on fighting to the death for a spot."

Sochi shook her head. "The world's in chaos, and you're worried about a little fight?"

Adon shrugged. "Maybe they're all just a bunch of alarmists? The waters will eventually recede, Sochi. There are probably other landmasses high enough above sea level. Besides..." He knocked on the wood-paneled galley wall. "...this boat is pretty sturdy. We could live here for years if we had to."

The motor purred softly as Adon expertly maneuvered *The Star Gazer* around several abandoned boats, most of them no longer seaworthy, and into the ocean. They'd be at the location in less than an hour.

Neither of them turned around to look at the devastation that was once a thriving city.

Sochi adjusted the diving mask and oxygen line. None of those so-called experts had thought to look off the coast of San Diego for Mayan ruins. Not for alien ones, either. If she didn't have the amulet, she doubted she'd be able to find the way. It was a transmission device, she discovered, as images began to appear in her mind after they dove off the side of *The Star Gazer* and swam toward a teetering pile of underwater boulders, some of which had been shaken loose during the last major quake.

There was a cave down here—and they were going to find it!

Sochi and Adon couldn't help but notice that the surrounding area was strangely devoid of sea life. Not a single fish or a single shark. Barren kelp beds drifted with light swells. Sochi hoped there wasn't something bigger and nastier to worry about rising up from the depths. She'd watched *Surface* with Adon, and these days, anything seemed possible.

Adon had "The End of the World as We Know It" playing through his mind and was seriously considering they were both crazy for attempting this—no matter what—or who—Sochi's *abuelita* may have been. Sochi interrupted his end-of-the-world musings with an excited, slightly frantic "Come here" wave.

The amulet was pulsing brighter as they approached a rent in the rock face. As they paused outside the opening, a beacon response glowed from inside.

Excited, but still cautious, Adon gestured that he'd go first. Sochi shook her head, pushed ahead of him. She couldn't fit through with her tank on, so she started to shrug it off.

Adon grabbed at her, tried to slip the tank back on, then realized she was right. They wouldn't fit through with them on.

But what if they ran out of air before they made it all the way inside? What if they got stuck, their air ran out, and—the most horrifying of all, Adon realized—what if they'd braved this possibility only to discover it was a dead-end, a beacon that called out through the centuries, programmed by beings who didn't know their underwater transport system had been destroyed?

He wasn't used to thinking negatively, but all in all, he was a realist, an explore-all-your-options kind of guy. Adon watched as Sochi swam through the opening, the tank clunking along the sides of the tunnel. He thought of giant sea worms, and despite the warmth of the water, he felt a chill shudder through his thermal suit. He waited a minute, then followed close behind her.

Relief flooded their minds when they discovered the tunnel was much shorter than when it first appeared and opened up into a somewhat large cave. A phosphorescent light was being emitted through the rock floor. Pulling themselves out of the water onto the cave floor, they joined hands as they carefully walked through the pristine silence.

Until Sochi cried out, grabbed her head.

"What's wrong?" Adon pulled Sochi toward him.

"There's this horrendous churning sound in my head. A high-pitched whine."

She breathed through it, and within moments, it passed. Adon mentally crossed himself, hoping this wasn't the first of many ordeals. It was odd how it hadn't affected him. More evidence, perhaps, that Sochi was the only person meant to be here.

Seeing an opening toward the back of the small cave, they quickened their pace, passed through a short passage into a huge cavern. Sochi and Adon stopped abruptly, gasped in unison.

There, right in front of them, in large, open vaults, were gigantic bats out of someone's worst nightmare. Within moments, sensing their arrival, two of the bats floated out of their vaults, hovered, and extended their wings.

Sochi and Adon both trembled, clutching each other. Sochi whimpered, buried her head in Adon's chest, her body wracked with chills.

A pale blue mist was released into the cavern, and their fear subsided, replaced by a deep sense of euphoria. Sochi didn't feel the razor-thin tubes penetrate deep into the veins in her neck, her wrists, her groin. She struggled to breathe as black wings surrounded her, then cocooned her in impenetrable darkness, a penetrating chill.

Sochi heard her grandmother's voice in her mind. "Let the Camazotz's blood flow into and through you. Let your blood merge with its blood." She allowed herself to let go and drifted into the flow of blood, her shivering eventually subsiding.

Adon watched in commingled horror and fascination as the metamorphosis began. The Camazotz's black wings surrounded his Sochi, melded with her. The only comparison Adon could make was the Irish tales of Selkies, how they could remove their skins, walk among and live as humans — but this was that tale in reverse.

Sochi was hooked up to the bat! Was it a parasite and she the host? The other way around? What if she couldn't return to normal again? As if anything would ever again be normal.

"This is the only way," she whispered into his mind. "The only way we can return home. Please —"

"But I'm not like you. My family's Portuguese, not Mayan. What if something goes wrong?"

"It won't," she spoke within his mind. "See... One of them came for you."

He turned away from Sochi to the other Camazotz hovering before him, its wingspan at least forty feet. He took a deep breath, clenched his eyes, and shuddered as the process began... His thoughts drifted away as his blood was drained from his body, as new Camazotzian blood coursed through his veins, and his blood, his human blood, was filtered through the Camazotz and back to him. An alien transfusion, he mused, his sense of irony mingled with fear.

For a moment, Adon wondered whether their thoughts would be mingled with the Camazotz as well. If he would see as—and what—the Camazotz saw. His body jerked, spasmed, then he drifted toward a drugged sleep.

Neither Sochi nor Adon knew how long they'd been asleep—or had they been in a sort of hibernation? Stasis? Both were awakened almost simultaneously by a whirring ping, like an internal alarm. They opened their eyes to an inky blackness suffused with multi-faceted shards of light.

It's like looking through a kaleidoscope, Soch, Adon thought.

Sochi was silent, marveling at the sight before her. She felt the Camazotz turn to the left, where The Seven Sisters were gathered to welcome her—to welcome them—home.

THE DARK LORD OF THE MARTIAN CANALS

Michael McCarty

"Earth is a long, long way from here," the female bartender said to the patron at the end of the bar.

"Uh, what?" said the longhaired guy.

"I thought you might be looking for Earth." She pointed to the dark sky in the glass ceiling. The entire sky could be seen clearly because the building looked more like a giant greenhouse than a drinking establishment.

"Oh, I was," he said.

"It's over there." She pointed to what looked like a star on the far horizon. When he turned to look, he could see down her jumpsuit, which was halfway unzipped. She wore no bra, so most of her lovely, shapely breasts could be seen.

"Nice," he said.

"My name is Sapphire Jones, the bartender and owner of The Watering Hole, the favorite dive bar on the red planet and its moons. But everyone just calls me Sapphy."

"Sapphire, like the gemstone?"

"You know your rocks. Are you one of the geologists they sent here to study the mineral deposits in the canals?" She pushed back the bangs of her light brown hair.

"No, I just studied Earth Science in high school. The name is Leonard Beck. Everybody calls me Lenny. I'm the entertainment Earth sent up here. I'm a day early. Just wanted to scope out the place."

"Oh," Sapphy said, a little disappointed. Geologists made a lot more than musicians did on the red planet. "The place may not be much, but it's the only place you can get alcohol on this moon or on Mars. This is the bar. We have over three-hundred Earth beers. That is the stage near the center of the room." She pointed to the platformed area with a fake brick wall behind it. "The bathrooms are over there. Next to the bathroom is the janitor's closet. And next to the janitor's closet is a greenroom, where you can suit up and tune up."

"Oh. Okay." Lenny smiled. "So, where's the Chronicle Motel?"

"Good Lord," Sapphy sighed. "They're putting you there. Which Level?"

"Level zero point one, the basement."

"Which room?"

"L seven."

She sighed again. "I'm in L nine. We'll be neighbors. I hope you won't bang your groupies too loud. I need my sleep."

"I don't think you have to worry about that. I play old Earth songs from the nineteen-sixties, seventies, and eighties. Ladies usually don't throw their panties at musicians playing those relic tunes."

"With the price of underwear these days, I don't blame them. Ordering undies from Earth is pricey."

They laughed.

"Let me buy you a drink," Sapphy said.

"I don't know," Lenny said. "I just got in from Earth, and I'm a little woozy already."

"Get enough alcohol in me, Big Boy, and I'll show my Earth undies," she said with a wink.

"I suppose a nightcap wouldn't kill either of us."

"What will you have?"

"What's a popular Mars drink?"

"Lotus juice with a splash of blood orange juice."

"What's that?"

"Blood orange is a fruit from Earth."

"I know that. I mean lotus juice."

"Oh," she said. "I forgot. You're new here. The lotus flower grows here on Phobos. It produces a juice that can be turned into alcohol, a lot stronger than the booze on Earth."

"I'm game."

She sliced up the blood orange, added the lotus juice to the blender, and turned on the mixer. After a few moments, she poured them both a drink.

"Cheers."

They clinked their glasses together.

There were several empty glasses on the bar.

"I told you I shouldn't have so many drinks," Lenny slurred the words. "The room's spinning; I don't think I can make it back to my room."

"Do you have your passkey?"

He nodded.

"Give it to me."

He handed the key card over to Sapphy.

"Grab your duffle bag and lean on me, Big Boy. I'll get you back to your room."

He grabbed the duffle bag and leaned on her, and she walked them down the long corridor together.

"Luckily, you don't weigh that much, and we don't have that far to go," she said as they took a left turn.

"Here's your Room, L seven." She stuck the card into the card reader, and the door slid open.

There wasn't much in the room. A TV, a sofa, a kitchenette, and a bathroom. His guitar had been delivered before he arrived.

In the middle of the room was a mattress.

She eased him down onto the bedding.

"Do you need help undressing?"

"No. But if you want to undress me, I wouldn't mind."

"Okay."

She took off his T-shirt, boots, and pants. He wore only a pair of black briefs, which she pulled off. She unzipped out of her jumpsuit. She was lying; she wasn't wearing any underwear. She knelt beside him, opened her mouth to form a perfect O, and engulfed his engorged member. Despite all the alcohol, he was getting hard fast.

She mounted him, straddling him like a cowgirl at a rodeo. Unlike a typical Earth bronco rider, she lasted a long, long time. Both were covered in sweat when they finally climaxed together.

She cuddled beside him, listening to his heart pound like a heavy metal drum solo.

"That was amazing," he finally said.

"It's been a while." She zipped up her jumpsuit. "I'm going home to get a little shuteye. My son leaves for school in about four hours. I gotta make him breakfast, too."

He tried to hide his surprise. "What's your kid's name."

"Donovan."

Shortly after Sapphire left, Leonard drifted into sleep, and he had the strangest dream:

Lenny was walking in the darkness; the absence of light was total. A big, red moon obscured by clouds was suddenly visible, and it was no longer dark. He also noticed he was standing beside a big, red building. It was still murky, but he could see it was enormous.

He heard a noise, like the baaing of goats. He turned around, and in the shadows, he saw a man. From the neck down, he looked like an athletic young man in his early twenties. Above the neck, he had a goat's head, complete with horns. His eyes glowed an eerie shade of green. The only non-goat thing on his head was his

teeth, which looked like steel fangs. He pointed to Lenny. "Leave!"
he bleated.

The next night, Lenny stepped onto the stage with his red acoustic guitar. He sat on the barstool next to the microphone stand.

He wore a T-shirt emblazoned with *Dark Side of the Moon*'s iconic album cover on it, which was released by Pink Floyd about a century ago.

"My name is Lenny Beck. I'm going to play a lot of songs from the nineteen-sixties, seventies, and eighties. This is a song I wrote called 'Dangerous.' I hope you like it."

He played a couple dozen notes on the guitar and began singing.

"It's dangerous to dream about you.
It's dangerous to want to kiss you,
but with the stars shining bright,
and the hazy moonlight,
it almost seems like the right thing to do.

It's dangerous for you to stay.
It's dangerous for my feelings to stray,
but in the darkness of the night,
with your eyes shining bright,
it almost seems like the right thing to do.

It's dangerous to love you.
It's dangerous, you know it's true.
But with nobody home,
and the two of us alone,
it almost seems like the right thing to do.

Our love holds no bounds.
We got to stand our grounds.
Because it's the right thing to do.
Dangerous, oh so dangerous.
It's dangerous, so dangerous."

For the next two hours, he played songs by The Beatles, ELO, The Eagles, and The Cars. It went over great with the audience, of course, because they were desperate for any live music and lucky to get an entertainer once or twice a year.

Like the night before, Sapphy ended up in Lenny's room. He took off his clothes. She unzipped her jumpsuit, revealing a pair of skimpy black panties.

"Wow," he said.

She slid them to the floor and lay on the mattress, face down.

"I'm exhausted," she said.

"Yeah, you were running your ass off."

"Jenny and Katrina called in sick, and we were balls to the wall all night."

"I suppose I could wait until tomorrow night."

"If you don't mind, how about doing it from behind?"

He stood up and got behind her. "I wouldn't mind. I wouldn't mind at all."

Outside the room, lying on the sandy ground were three teen-agers: Donovan Jones, Dana Bognanno, and Johnny Navarro. The girl was looking in the window with her night vision goggles. She handed them to Johnny, who looked through them for a moment before handing them to Donovan.

"The Dark Lord of the Martian Canals was right," Donovan said softly. "I don't see what she sees in him. The long hair, yuck."

He handed the goggles over to Dana. "I kinda think it's sexy."

"Remember what the Dark Lord said?" Donovan asked.

"No fornication until the birth of the New Messiah," Johnny, Dana, and Donovan chanted quietly in unison.

"Good."

"How long do you think that will be?" Dana asked.

Donovan shrugged.

When they were finished, Sapphy slid her black panties on. Lenny lay next to her, resting his head near her breasts.

"I'm on the Welcome Committee," Sapphy said. "I was supposed to give you the welcome speech two days ago."

"Believe me, you made me feel welcome. Plenty."

"Do you mind if I give you the speech now?"

"Sure. Go for it."

"Welcome to Phobos, one of two moons of Mars; it's the largest of the two moons and circles the red planet three times a day. It's an oddly shaped moon, like a potato, and has low gravity. The lack of gravity makes it easy to take a stroll, but keep it slow. If you go too fast, you could be thrown from the surface.

"The domed city that we're in is called Anamosa. It really isn't a city, more of a village, with a population of three hundred. We have a police department, fire department, farmers, and teachers. The town is divided into three parts: The farming division, the military training and construction division, and the housing/education/living division.

"Outside the domed city is a big, red building, which is now abandoned. It was the Anamosa Science Building. Because it was built on a fault line, it was uninhabitable."

"Where is this science building?" Lenny asked.

"Near the canals. You didn't see it when your ship landed?"

"No, but I think I might have seen it in a nightmare."

"Oh," she paused. "If this is bothering you, I don't have to continue."

"Go ahead."

"Everyone who comes to Anamosa will get a contract, two, five, or ten years. After the terms of the contract, you can renew it or go back to Earth. The contract can be terminated if a family member dies or you get married or you can buy it out for the original terms and conditions."

"How long is your contract?"

"I have a ten-year contract. It isn't due for another five months. I will most likely renew it."

"Instead of renewing your contract, let's get married and go back to Earth."

"I don't know," Sapphy said reluctantly. "We just met. You haven't even met my son yet."

"I have a great condo in New York City overlooking Central Park."

"I don't know."

"What's your son like?"

"He's tall, dark hair. Good at school. He and a couple of kids from school have a club together."

"That's good. What kind of club?"

"Maybe club isn't a good word. It is more of a cult, I guess. They worship The Dark Lord of the Martian Canals."

"What are the canals?"

"The canals on Mars and Phobos. It's a long story."

"Do they ever describe what the Dark Lord looks like?"

"I've never seen him, but what my son told me, I heard he has a goat's head. Not sure if he's wearing the head of a goat or if it is a mask or whatever. But I heard he has glowing eyes and sharp, metal teeth."

"I want to meet your son."

"You don't have a show tonight. I'll make us dinner. You can come over and meet Donovan."

That night, Lenny took a hot shower. Because of water rations, the shower was only two minutes long, but he made good use of those two minutes. He wore a Depeche Mode "Personal Jesus" T-shirt and his nicest pair of jeans.

Sapphy, Donovan, and Lenny sat at the small card table, eating their dinner, which was a roasted Mars chicken. It was larger than an Earth chicken, but the meat was tougher. They also had a salad and mineral water.

They ate in silence. Finally, Lenny broke the silence.

"I'm Lenny," he said. "I'm a musician."

"I know," Donovan said nonplused. "I don't like your hair. Too long."

Lenny looked at Donovan's haircut, which was cut military style, close to the skull.

"Your mom said you belong to The Dark Lord of the Martian Canals. Is it some kind of youth church group?"

He nodded but didn't look up and kept eating.

"Where's the church located?" Lenny asked.

"The old science building. Do you want to go there?"

"Yes."

After they had finished dinner, Donovan took Lenny to the basement and showed him the astronaut suits they would have to wear to go outside of the dome. Donovan's fit comfortably. Lenny's was a little tight and his helmet was hard to see out of.

The abandoned science building was even bigger than in Lenny's dream. Its blood-red color blended in with the dark, reddish skies.

The interior of the science building was dark, except for a few battery-powered lanterns placed around a giant gold statue of a man with a goat head. Lenny estimated it was close to nine feet tall and nine feet wide.

Lenny looked at the sculpture. Thinking it was painted gold, he tapped on it and discovered it was real gold. He wondered how the hell they could get that much gold up here.

"What is that?" Lenny said, pointing at the statue.

"The Dark Lord."

Lenny stopped in his tracks. It looked like the evil creature in his dream.

"We meet at last," the Dark Lord said, stepping from behind his own statue.

Speechless, Lenny took a step back. The Dark Lord scared the hell out of him. He looked like something out of an H.R. Giger painting, with the background forming the darkest of nightmares.

"You will not take Brother Donovan away from us and return to Earth."

Lenny's mouth was too dry to talk. How did this guy know all of this? Finally, he croaked, "Donovan? That isn't going to happen for some time. I can explain—"

"The time for talk is over! Get him now," the Dark Lord said as he pointed his finger at Lenny. "Time to begin the Master Plan."

"Master Plan! Master Plan! Master Plan!" The three teenagers charged him, pulling out sharp knives and stabbing him in a frenzy. They say in space, no one can hear you scream. This was true here, too. His screams of pain couldn't be heard outside of the domed city.

The knives pierced his protective suit, making him lose precious oxygen. The jagged blades penetrated his flesh repeatedly and the screaming soon stopped. Lenny staggered briefly, like a drunk leaving a bar after closing time. He was out of oxygen and bleeding profusely. He collapsed on the ground, dead.

"It is time for the rebirth." The Dark Lord made a fist with his hand. "Time for the coming of the New Messiah."

"The New Messiah." The three teenagers held their bloody knives together as they chanted.

Sapphy was in a deep sleep when she felt something touch her arm, waking her.

"Lenny?" When she opened her eyes, she saw her son was pinning her arm down.

"Donovan, what are you doing?"

He didn't answer. She could not move the other arm; Dana was kneeling on it.

"What's going on?"

No one responded. She shrieked as the blanket was yanked away and her panties were ripped from her body.

She struggled futilely as a naked, goat-headed man spread her legs and positioned himself between them.

"The New Messiah will soon emerge!" chanted the teenagers, their mantra inaudible over Sapphy's screams.

The Dark Lord entered her...

SISTERS OF THE BLOOD MOON

Terrie Leigh Relf

Miri watched the dense indigo fog gather and swirl just beyond the cavern's protective force field. Soola's third moon, Poora, had finally risen into the night sky, and she recoiled at the increasing violence of the waves as they thrashed against the outer barricade. The season of tides had begun early this year, and she pondered the precarious balance of her life.

Despite the controlled climate functions, Miri felt cold and involuntarily shivered, causing her pale blue skin to darken. She wore a long vermillion shift of Mora spider silk that clung to her like a second skin. Her thick, dark blue hair was wound into an elaborate bun and secured with hair pins carved from local wood.

Her childhood friend, Tura, was about to arrive on an official Trilune matter. Miri knew it must be urgent; braving travel—even by starslip—was almost unheard of during this season.

There were other matters that seemed to defy explanation, such as her recurring dreams. These were a sure sign of visions, but without the offering of blood, she wasn't certain.

The T'ar-el usually needed the offering to see beyond the four corners of the galaxy, beyond the three times of past, present, and future, into the realm where possibilities co-existed before set in motion. It was that fertile ground the Sisters of the Blood Moon were able to manipulate by seeing possibilities as they were unveiled in multiple dimensions. This was a responsibility reserved for, and borne by, the Sisterhood.

At first, the dreams had been peaceful scenes of water lapping within her sanctuary's subterranean pools. There had been an unusual stone archway, though, and rather than framing Soola's angry, storm-filled sky, there was a serene blue vista wrought with the light, opalescent clouds—and a single moon barely discernable in the distance.

Once she noticed this odd landscape, the dreams shifted. The single archway became many, each larger than the last, so that she gazed through a tunnel unfurling before her like the inner coil of a tidal wave. She walked across smooth, dry stones that arose from the water, but these soon became slippery.

Miri looked at her bare feet, saw an unfamiliar plant, bent over to touch and smell it. While unusual, it had a pleasant aroma. Fresh. Fertile. It was rare for her to have such strong sensory experiences within a dream. Even the scent of the air was unlike any she'd smelled before – and that taste on her tongue, what was it? A form of salt?

There had been someone with her in the dream. While she couldn't see them, she could hear short, shallow breaths, the unmistakable beat of a single heart.

Given her training, Miri could awaken herself at any time, yet she felt compelled to remain in this dreamscape, to see that brilliant blue sky, that brilliant single moon that hung low on the horizon.

Just before first light, another version of this dream had been unveiled. The path she walked became labyrinthian and wended around like a poochi bug through moist soil. Finally, it opened into a cavern that bore the horrible stench of death and decay.

Had she journeyed here before on the slipstream of an offering's blood? Could this be her future? Tura's? Why couldn't she see more? What did this signify?

It wasn't like her to doubt her abilities, her purpose, but how long had it been since someone had come to Soola for a matter of major import?

Perhaps her world was changing, and the Sisterhood would become obsolete. Who really wanted—or needed—to know their future? Perhaps it was best to allow the lives of others to be unveiled without answers.

Or perhaps they had learned to read the future for themselves...

It was good to question one's place—and purpose—in the universe, Miri mused but realized she was being indulgent. She needed to be prepared to help Tura and Trilune, she reminded herself as the telltale reverberations of a descending starslip reached her awareness.

The crystalline walls were often like a scrying pond to her, but right now, with her mind awhirl with too many questions, all she wanted to do was lean against the cool, smooth surface. She willed herself to be calm, directed all three of her hearts to slow down to barely a perceptible beat, then extended her awareness to the sounds, scents, and the landing pool...the hum of the approaching starslip...the scent of mora blossom tea brewing in the kitchen... and woven throughout, the longing for a change in her routine... for flesh against flesh... for Tura's flesh against hers.

"What is it you require of me today, dear friend?" Miri whispered as the starslip, guided by an energetic stream, descended through the partially artificial cavern roof, settling with barely a splash into the landing pool.

She walked briskly down the short, stone corridor that opened into the cavern housing the landing pool. Normally, she would have her attendants meet an entourage, but this visit was special. She arrived just as the door hissed open to reveal three Trilune guards wearing the standard blue artificial skin over their massive physiques. In the center of their all-terrain uniforms, just below the collar, was the Trilune crest: three pale gray circles positioned at equal distances over a dark, curved line.

The first guard moved to stand to the left of the opening, the second to the right, while the third guard extended his hands to assist Tura from the craft. Miri could hear the rapid fall of footsteps as several of her attendants ran the distance from the main quarters. They murmured apologies that Miri waved away.

Tura, now on the somewhat solid ground of the cavern floor, released the guard's hands. She approached Miri, her hands raised to form crescent moons, leaving the suggestion of empty space to represent the Blood of the Moon. As a young girl, Tura had been tested and found not to have the gift. They had drunk their first blood together, but it had been Miri who had transformed, Miri who had seen, so Tura had become an official attendant, part advisor, part messenger, part whatever else was needed.

Miri returned the greeting, and the two friends looked deeply into each other's eyes. So alike in outward appearances, so different beneath the surface, yet they were still connected despite the different paths their lives had taken. These paths often intertwined and overlapped, much like the lunar eclipse of a distant sun. The vision of a lunar eclipse filled her eyes once she had drunk the offering of blood.

The guard who had assisted Tura re-entered the starslip and returned with what first appeared to be children. Upon closer inspection, Miri realized they were no longer children, but had naturally pale, smooth skin. There were four females with hair the hue of starlight and almond-shaped eyes that glowed bronze in the wan light. The male had a close-shaven head, its smooth surface glistening. Unlike the females', his eyes were dark blue...nearly obsidian... Miri gasped in recognition.

They seemed dazed from their journey, and Miri hoped they had not been drugged, as their blood would be tainted—and she needed their life's elixir to be pure when summoning the sight in the Star Chamber.

Her eyes felt dry, so she closed them. A vivid dreamscape unveiled within her mind. She moaned as a wave of vertigo passed through her. She reached out involuntarily to steady herself. Which of the four females was sending to her? She opened her eyes, looked at each of them in turn. Could there be Blood Moon Sisters on other worlds?

The male had closed and clenched his eyes. There was something special about this one. It wasn't just that his eyes resembled hers. She sensed he had the sight as well. She had never heard of a male so endowed, so she shrugged this thought away, replaced it with what she knew to be true. Once chosen, she and the offerings were bound. Their memories to hers, their thoughts to hers, their senses to hers.

Miri closed her eyes again, saw the curved entryway that now opened into the Star Chamber. The walls began to seep water, then swirled with blood. Bodies rose to the surface. So many bodies... their eyes vacant, unseeing.

How many moments had passed while she witnessed this vision? She opened her eyes again, glanced at the male, decided he would be the first. As if sensing her gaze, his eyes fluttered open and he looked at her without blinking, without fear. His full lips turned up into a smile. Did he not realize what was about to happen?

An odd sensation arose in her. Fear? Panic? To whom did it belong? Tura? The offerings? No! It was her own fear, and that was unnerving, as the unknown was part of her daily existence.

Tura was used to the long pauses. It was ever thus with the Sisterhood, and especially with Miri. "You realize we have come on a matter of urgency," Tura finally said. She bowed slightly in respect.

Miri returned the bow but longed to embrace her friend.

"Yes, it is not often we receive The Offering of Five." She allowed her gaze to rest briefly on the youth who remained standing with the guard.

Tura cradled one of her long, slender hands within the other. It was a technique taught by the Sisters of the Blood Moon and was very effective when needing to still—or gather—one's thoughts.

"What urgent matter is this?" Miri asked, keeping her head bowed slightly. "Perhaps your attendants would like to rest. It has been a long journey—and the young ones, they look like they could sleep for several turns."

"Thank you, yes." Tura nodded to the guards, said something in a language Miri didn't know. They darted looks at each other, seemed to hesitate, then motioned for the five to walk ahead of them. The male turned to look at Miri. Their eyes locked for but a moment, and she felt her body shudder in response.

Miri's attendants, three young females from Soola's smallest moon, Bejar, followed behind the two guards, while the third remained behind. It was a short walk to the communal area, where there were thick floor coverings and cushions. A pale light emanated from small alcoves carved within the stone and crystal walls. The room was comfortable, if not comforting. The attendants busied themselves with pouring tea and preparing a light meal of fruit and honey while Miri and Tura, a guard in tow, continued walking toward the room that led to the Star Chamber.

Once Miri and Tura relaxed on a couch, a guard took his position in the entryway, his broad back nearly blocking the entrance. It was a small room and was usually cooler than the rest of the subterranean habitat. Once they climbed the narrow stairs leading to the even smaller chamber above, they would have a clear view of the night sky. She wondered if the three moons would be visible tonight or if the dense fog would shroud their view.

"There is a planet near the Hauran system," Tura began, "which has been sending probes into deep space. We have managed to shut most of them down. Now they drift like so many dried poochi bug husks on the wind."

"Ah, so you come for advice on interplanetary relations..."

"In part. These five come from that system, and so we offer them to you, to see as they see, to feel as they feel, to know as they know."

"But they are not from Haura—and they are so young. How much could they possibly know—"

"They are much older than they appear, my friend." Tura started to say something else.

"You do not come during the season of the tides to tell me of satellite probes that have been decommissioned."

"No, I do not. There is more..." She glanced toward the guard's immobile back. "These five... They claim there will be some sort of interplanetary event, that we will feel this, even on Soola. The male at the end, do you recall him?"

"Yes, I do," Miri said, feeling a gathering chill. Those bodies floating. Those faceless bodies.

"He claims to have seen it." Tura looked meaningfully in Miri's direction. "A vision of this horrible event. An alignment of the moons. Once the Blood Moon rises, it will remain—or some such holocaust. How can this be? We wouldn't have given him any credence, but he claims you are an integral part of his vision. He described you..."

Miri stood up abruptly. "I have seen this flood—not on Soola—but on another world with a single moon. I believe I have seen it through his eyes. Bodies everywhere. Bloated. Faceless bodies. How can this be? How can he be doing this—how can I without the offering of his blood?"

Tura reached out to grasp her friend's hands, to pull her down beside her on the couch. "You must drink of him first to find out if what he says is true—there's more..."

Miri leaned in closer, turned toward Tura, who continued to whisper. "His name is Danyal, and he is some sort of scientist from a system the Haurans call *Alpha Centauri*, near what they call the Pleiades. The Seven Sisters, Miri. There is a connection to us—the Sisterhood."

Miri allowed this information to flow through her mind. Seven Sisters—an alignment that remains...scientists brought as offerings...

"Worlds die and worlds are born, even reborn, but if what you say is true, what can I possibly see to alter such a future?"

"I really do not understand their science—or ours, for that matter. What I do know is that not long after their probes were shut down, a craft bearing these five was detected. They were brought to Trilune headquarters. It was difficult to translate their language—and their intent—but—"

"But an alignment—" Miri began.

"It's not catastrophic in itself. Yes, I know this, Miri, but there's more to it. This is what you need to see for us. If what they say is true, then this is a future we need to acknowledge. Our lives may not be at stake here, but what of the Coalition of Planets? What happens to one affects us all—"

"You, of all beings, know the face of hope, Tura. It is your strength." Miri took her best friend's hand, drew her into a close embrace. Tura sighed as Miri stroked the back of her neck, pressed her closer.

"I wish that we could lie together before the offering, Miri. It has been too long since we've been in each other's arms," Tura whispered as she pulled away, one of her hands still draped around Miri's lower back.

Miri turned toward the guard's immobile form, leaned forward to rest her forehead against Tura's. "As do I."

"It is always thus, is it not? That we must serve others before ourselves?"

The Star Chamber was a circular tower near the uppermost section of the cavern. If not for the protective, yet transparent, membrane that covered it, the room would be open to the elements. Soola's three moons suffused the chamber with light, the Blood Moon's eerie shadow only slightly obscuring it.

The ritual dais was in the room's center. There was a series of three steps in each of the four directions that led up to it. The dais was slightly bowled, with an opening at the center to receive any blood that would spill. Around the opening was a decorative pattern: Two opalescent crescent moons carved around a hematite Blood Moon, its outer ring composed of faceted crimson stones. It was here Miri stood, waiting for her attendants to bring Danyal.

Since the ceremonial area took up nearly the entire space, large ovals had been hewn into the surrounding rock wall, each culminating into a curved seat. This was where Tura waited for the ceremony to begin, trying to ignore the pungent odor that made her slightly nauseated. She remembered the first time she had inhaled this scent—when she drank blood with Miri. It had sickened her then as well.

She had known then, as she knew now, that in many ways, she was nearly the same as one born totally blind. Without the sight known to the T'ar-el and to the Sisters of the Blood Moon, she could only stand vigil when blood was spilled, when death inevitably came.

Miri's attendants finally entered the Star Chamber with Danyal, who was wearing a long tunic made of plain Mora spider silk. The three Trilune guards remained at a distance as one attendant led him to the foot of the dais, motioned for him to climb the three steps toward Miri, who took his hand and led him to the dais's center.

Miri felt Danyal's hands in hers, saw them pale against her darker flesh. She closed her eyes, and he did the same. She had not even drunk from him and could already feel the burn of his blood within her, the bloodburn that would unlock his mind to hers.

Tura raised her hands, then closed them together, thus beginning the ritual. "What do you see?" Her voice resonated through the Star Chamber space.

Miri opened her eyes and Tura stifled a gasp. No matter how many times she had witnessed the change coming upon one of the Sisters of the Blood Moon, she was never prepared for it. Dark eyes remained dark, but like a solar eclipse, a ring of scarlet surrounded them. But the most frightening aspect was how the outer circle seemed to ripple with flames.

"What do you see?" Tura asked again.

The back of Miri's neck began to burn as sharp, opalescent tendrils emerged from her spine, breaking through her skin to pierce Danyal's bare neck. She could hear his sharp intake of breath as the needle-fine filaments penetrated his flesh, sought the labyrinth of veins that would release their vital essence.

"What do you see?" Tura called out, the ritual words drifting through Miri's awareness. She sensed rather than saw Danyal's blood flowing through her veins, releasing its knowledge to her.

What do you see? What do you see? What do you see? The words echoed in her mind.

It was dark at first, then crimson flickered at the edges of her vision, crimson bursting from the center of the darkness. Crimson, crimson, all was crimson.

She cried out, arched her back, and began to fall, the filaments still embedded within Danyal, still pulsing with his blood. The process hadn't weakened him, as he caught her in his arms and gently eased her to the dais.

"Poison! He has poisoned her!" Then another said, "No, she still breathes..."

The moment moved slowly with Miri. No words were adequate to describe her vision. The ground writhed and split, molten flames and red-hot rocks spewing from deep fractures. Then waves, great torrents of water roaring and pounding, until all that remained was an impenetrable stillness.

Miri's flesh began to burn and itch at the same time—it was maddening! She felt as if she were writhing on the ground, and yet those who surrounded her beheld a still form. She saw through their eyes—through all their eyes.

Their world is dying.

Then a buzzing, like a swarm of poochi bugs when their hive was breached. Could another starslip be arriving? But no, the sound was coming from deep within her.

Her skin began to ripple as her pores enlarged, releasing tendrils so thin that they would be transparent if not for their opalescent fire. Where her flesh was not exposed, they pierced through the thin fabric of her robe.

The attendants backed down the steps, called out, "What do we do?" Everyone was frozen in place, barely able to breathe, as they witnessed the writhing mass of tendrils emerging from Miri's back and spine, snaking out, trembling in the air, recoiling before striking out again.

Danyal had been forgotten for a moment; the words he called out were alien to their minds. They sensed he meant Miri no harm, so no one stopped him as he lay down next to her and pulled her closer to himself.

Now face-to-face, Miri's eyes parted for a moment at his touch. She could see his eyes burning with the same flame as her own, but where hers were obsidian with a crimson circle, his were now crimson and ringed with the darkest shade of night. She sighed, closed her eyes, and surrendered, her body relaxing against his until she felt him stiffen to receive the sharp filaments that began to weave together into a pulsing mass. His blood to her, hers to him, as if they were a singular being.

Miri's attendants, Tura, and the guards moved as far away as possible, given the small confines. None of them had ever seen the offering of blood cause such a transformation before.

Inside the latticework of pulsing veins, Danyal and Miri shared a single vision.

It was like her dreams, only more vivid. First, the brilliant blue sky with a single moon. Then darkness followed by immense waves bearing the bodies of too many dead. Habitats above ground trembled, wobbled before being crushed. The ground shook and crumbled.

Soola and her three moons weren't on the brink of destruction. It was another world that would soon cease to exist, another world whose beings deserved to be saved.

Show me more...

Danyal showed her a vision: One of his planet's starships heading toward Haura, waiting in geosynchronous orbit around the planet. Then, a fleet of Trilune starslips breaching space to join them.

But where would they all go? How could they be convinced to leave?

Danyal showed her a dying world, its remaining inhabitants huddled together, barely living. He showed her one group of these beings looking to the sky, not in fear, but with hope, holding on to each moment, each breath, as a sign that help would arrive.

We are that hope, Danyal said within her mind as the tendrils began to release their grip. They slid effortlessly from his body, and rather than return to Miri's spine, they grew pale and fell away as dry husks.

Miri and Danyal open their eyes in unison and lay there motionless before attempting to rise. Miri's attendants rushed to help her, but she waved them away.

Danyal stirred first, stood, weakened from the ordeal but still able to pull Miri to her feet. She leaned against him, searched for, found Tura among the expectant faces surrounding them.

"The people of Haura need us," was all that Miri said, but it was enough to alter all their fates and futures.

RED SNOW

Michael McCarty

It started with the cold front. Bitterly frigid temperatures swept across the United States from north to south and east to west. Zero degrees, below zero degrees, and the wind chill factor even more wintry. This weird drop in temps caused inexplicable events to happen—iguanas began to freeze and fall from trees in Florida, frozen sharks and whales washed ashore in Georgia, rats froze in Chicago, and garter snakes froze on the sidewalks of San Francisco.

Then came the snow, the interminable snow. It snowed and snowed and snowed. It didn't seem like it would ever end. Birds that migrated south for the winter died in droves. Orange trees in California stopped bearing fruit.

Then all the snow turned red; crimson snowflakes fell, making the sky look like it was bleeding. People had theories about it—red rain that froze, dust from Mars—nobody had time to find out the real reason because that was when the dead returned to life and feasted on the living...

Emma Erickson drove her Ford F-150 truck easily through the red snow. The roads in Rock Island, Illinois, had been salted but were still slick in spots. The F-150 plowed through the red, frosty slush to Hilltop Dry Cleaners without sliding too badly. The truck was the best thing she got from her ex. During bad weather, it was great for getting around, but normally the vehicle was too much of a gas guzzler, sucking down fuel like a dehydrated vampire.

She dreaded going to work today. The red snow made business slower, and because fellow worker, Charlotte Wellendorf, hadn't been at the cleaners for over a week, it meant she'd also have to fill in doing counterwork. Nothing against working the front, but she didn't know what to say to customers anymore. Everybody seemed to take offense to even the most innocent of comments. It seemed society was going backward these days, not forward.

Emma was about half a block from work when she started to slow down. Not because of the weather conditions, but what she saw in the parking lot—a red truck attached to a thirty-foot trailer, also in red, labeled with big block letters that read:

ROCK ISLAND FIRE DEPARTMENT: HAZARDOUS MATERIALS

She pulled into the parking lot, stopped, and dialed her boss, Hannah. As the phone rang, thoughts cascaded through her head: "W.T.F.? Why is a hazmat truck in front of work? Is it some kind of chemical spill? Is it safe to go inside?"

The questions remained unanswered because Hannah's phone went straight to voicemail.

"This is Emma," she said to the voicemail. "I'm in the parking lot at work. Give me a call back as soon as possible and let me know what the hell is going on."

Looked at her watch. Fifteen minutes before work started. Drumming her fingertips on the steering wheel. Waited and waited and waited. Looked at the watch once again. Five minutes before work started.

Looked up at the truck again and gingerly inched her truck past the hazmat vehicle. She pulled to the front of the cleaners, where Hannah's car was parked. Next to her boss's car was Patty's Beetle. That was as strange as seeing both doors to the shopfront wide open.

"Hannah!" Emma yelled. "Patty!" She walked through the front doors, scanning the lobby, front counter, backroom, and opened-door bathroom. She checked everywhere, including her office. No sign of them whatsoever.

"That's strange," she whispered to herself.

She dialed Hannah again. Same result—voicemail. She called Patty next—voicemail, too. Odd.

Her boss's car, Patty's car, and the semi were still at the cleaners.

There was still work to do. After working for the dry cleaners for the last two years, she knew the drill:

Press.

Steam.

Iron.

Fold.

Package.

Start over again.

She fired up the pressing machine and waited for the steam to get hot. The machine had been nicknamed "The Barbecue" because it reached temperatures up to 600 degrees Fahrenheit.

A video camera recorded the area where she pressed. Customers complained twice as much about lost clothing as damaged clothing, so her boss recorded everything and doubled down on the invoices to try to avoid this happening.

She heard a slurping sound, like someone sucking on a spaghetti dinner or drinking to get the last few drops from their slushie.

"Hannah! Patty!"

Still no answer.

She heard the slurping noise again. She listened closely and could tell it was coming from the backroom.

Emma went into the backroom. She could hear lapping and guzzling sounds from behind the steel door in the back. The back door hadn't been opened since she began working at the cleaners. Even on the hottest and most sultry days of summer, it remained locked because the business was in a high crime area and several other establishments had been robbed before.

She unlocked the door, opened it, and saw someone lying on the sidewalk in a puddle of blood and gore in the deep, red snow. It looked like Hannah was kneeling beside her, maybe applying bandages to the wound to stop the bleeding. Emma approached and saw that the person lying on the ground was her co-worker, Patty. Her boss was kneeling next to the body, not to help with first aid but to gnaw on bloody bits of flesh from her shredded neck.

Hannah turned and looked at Emma with no recognition in her dead eyes. Her boss's face was covered with blood and gore; her eyes were slightly white, no color in her pupils whatsoever.

Emma's stomach churned; she fought the urge to vomit. She had seen enough zombie movies and TV shows to know that Hannah was now one of the living dead. Emma turned toward the building; she had no traction in the slippery, blood-colored snow. She slipped and fell on her butt before reaching the door.

When she was first hired, Emma had to watch a training video about the dangers of PERC (a chemical known as perchloroethylene or tetrachloroethylene). There had been no instructions about how to respond when your boss turned into a flesh-eating zombie and was bent on making you breakfast.

Emma quickly tried to back up and instantly fell face forward on her stomach, sprawled out spread-eagled on the ground. From her Karate training, she knew she was close to helpless lying on her stomach. She could sense Hannah lurching toward her.

Emma spun onto her back and saw the zombie that had been her boss was coming toward her.

Emma drew her knees to her chest. As Hannah bent down to attack her, Emma slammed her feet into Hannah's chest, sending her backward into the deepening crimson snow.

Emma hoped and prayed that Hannah's skull had been fractured in the fall. Shivering, her clothes soaked, Emma nearly wept upon seeing Hannah struggling to her feet again.

"Dammit!" Emma said. "All I did was piss her off!"

Hannah reached for her feet.

Emma grabbed the gore-stained wrist and bent the arm backward. She knew it only took six pounds of pressure to break an elbow, so she kept pushing and pushing with all her weight against the arm until she heard a sickening snap. Hannah's arm was dangling in the air.

Emma quickly got up and ran back inside the building. She ran past the pressing machine to grab her purse and coat, but it was too late. Her boss grabbed her hair with her good arm, pulling her closer. Emma grabbed a pair of scissors lying next to the machine and pushed the blades into Hannah's hand; she let go.

Emma then pushed Hannah's head onto the scalding surface of the pressing machine. She heard the flesh searing against the red-hot metal. She thought she'd scream in pain, but instead stared with her dead yellow eyes. Then she slammed Hannah's head onto the red-hot surface and brought the pressing machine together, searing her superior's face. She pushed down on the equipment, harder and harder, until she heard the skull crack.

Hannah's body jerked around like a drunk frat boy tased by the police, then suddenly went flaccid.

Emma released the pressing machine, and her boss's limp body crumpled to the floor. She then ran to her truck, snatched the keys from her purse, and was about to open the door when she felt an icy grip on the back of her shoulder. She turned to see Patty standing behind her. Like the boss, she had become a zombie. Her neck oozed blood.

With the truck keys in her hand, Emma jabbed them into Patty's white eye. The eye turned bloody red as blood spurted from the open wound like a fountain.

Emma shoved her to the ground. She crammed the bloody key into the keyhole, unlocked and opened the door with the last smidgen of energy she could muster, jumped into the truck, and locked the door.

Filled with fear and feeling exhausted, Emma started the truck, shifted into drive, and floored the pedal. The vehicle slid and swerved on the parking lot pavement toward the street. Before she pulled onto 18th Avenue, she saw three zombie firemen blocking her path, but that was only temporary. The truck rammed into the trio of the undead, and they were quickly airborne, crashing and landing on the street. The whole scene looked like a horror movie about bowling a strike.

Emma didn't bother to see if the zombie firemen were going to get up or not because the truck was speeding down 18th Avenue as she made her escape. As she drove away, she looked at the red snow all over the ground and buildings and knew her world wasn't going to be the same anymore, but at least she wouldn't have to return to work again...

GREY WOLF, THE SKINWALKERS, AND THE SKY CLAN
Terrie Leigh Relf

It was a cold night, even for early spring, as Grey Wolf, or Grey, as his friends called him, made his way across the thick-packed earth toward the jagged base of Sangre de Cristos.

The moon was nearly full, and there was a spattering of stars to guide him. He remembered how his grandfather used to tell him stories of their people, the Cherokee, and how those stars were the campfires of their ancestors. His grandfather also talked of people who visited the Earth from beyond the stars. He called them Sky People, or the Sky Clan, but Grey always believed these stories were like the white man's fairy tales, just stories to entertain children and keep the elders busy. Whoever heard of people traveling from the stars? They could barely keep the trains and coaches running.

Until that flying ship had crashed last spring in Aurora, Texas… He hadn't seen it with his own eyes, but his grandfather said it was the Sky People come to visit.

The Sky People, according to his grandfather, would descend to the earth in beams of gold or silver light. They were tall, like the Cherokee, but their skin was pale, their hair long and white like snow, and their eyes were either blue like storm-ridden skies, or green like moss-covered rock. There was a part of him that wanted it to be true, that knew it had to be true.

He shivered again, tugged the fur-lined hat over his ears, rewound the long woolen scarf Miss Carmen had given him for luck. It was soft to the touch, a girl's scarf, he had joked, but since it was warm, he accepted the gift.

He'd been worried his friend, Armando, who also worked with him on the de la Madrid ranch, might get jealous of the gift. Armando was in love with Sr. de la Madrid's daughter, Miss Carmen, and it was clear she loved him as well. Her father, Esteban, didn't approve of them spending so much time together, as they weren't children anymore, and Miss Carmen was already spoken for.

The de la Madrids and the Websters owned adjoining ranches and had been friends since before their children were born. Miss Carmen was betrothed to the Webster's youngest son, Louis. Carmen hadn't gotten a choice in the matter, which Grey didn't think was fair. Louis was okay, and he liked him well enough, but Armando was his friend, and Grey was sad Armando couldn't marry the woman he loved.

But all that had changed the morning they found Louis's body.

Miss Carmen was horrified by what happened to Louis, and grieved for him, but Grey imagined she was secretly relieved. Even though she dutifully wore black dresses, covered her hair and face with a black lace scarf, and stayed inside the house, Armando told him they met secretly in the old barn.

Louis had died a horrible death. No one deserved to die like that. He'd been so young. Not even twenty summers. While Grey hadn't seen the body, he'd heard the men at the ranch talk. Louis had been found near a copse of trees with every inch of his flesh skinned away. He didn't know of any animal that could do such a thing.

"Skinwalkers," was whispered across the valley that was home to several ranches and farms just outside Santa Fe.

Skinwalkers.

Grey tried to laugh it away. He'd heard the elders whisper tales about the Navaho Skinwalkers, but these were just a legend, like the Sky People. A story told to scare children into being obedient. There had been some talk among the men at the ranch that there was a soldier who occasionally hung around, and maybe he did it. The man said he was just looking for honest work now that the war was over. Esteban had sent him away, said he drank too much, and his Carolina, may she rest in peace, wouldn't approve of a man like that being anywhere near their precious daughter.

But Louis hadn't been the first—or the last. Several more people from Webster's, and then Hodgkin's ranch, had disappeared, only to turn up a day or so later, mutilated beyond recognition. What type of blade could do that? And what manner of man could wield it?

Some said it could be one of the miners gone crazy in the hot sun and stifling heat. Even the old grandmothers whispered about *brujas* or medicine men working curses with shadow beings. Word traveled fast, and soon, accusations with them. It made Grey nervous. A crowd of men with fear gnawing at their minds and bellies might act before thinking. Innocent people would get hurt. Loved ones would be caught in the crossfire of misplaced revenge.

So, when Miss Carmen had told him and Armando the story about a woman who lived alone in the mountains, how she could help them, they drew straws to see who would make the journey to ask for her help.

Grey had drawn the short straw, and Miss Carmen was visibly relieved. Armando tried to act all macho, argued that he should be the one, as it was his woman making the request, but Grey insisted he stay behind. Someone needed to help protect Miss Carmen, didn't they? Besides, Grey admonished him, "I wouldn't be able to forgive myself if something happened to you, and Miss Carmen would never forgive me for surviving."

Grey took another swig of water from his skin, wiped his lips, then hung it back on his pack for the next part of the climb. The mountain was getting steeper, but it looked like Miss Carmen was right. There, about sixty feet or so ahead, was the ledge she had mentioned. It was a steep climb, but he could do it. He couldn't imagine a woman living all the way up here by herself, and for a moment, he wondered if she was a *bruja* of some kind. Even if she were, Miss Carmen wouldn't send him to her without good reason. He would be strong and call upon the ancestors to protect him.

Miss Carmen had drawn him a small map, but since she'd never been here herself, how did she know it was accurate? Still, he trusted her. Besides, when Carmen's mother was on her deathbed, she made Carmen promise to seek out this woman's help if anything bad ever happened.

Grey was curious about how Miss Carmen's mother knew this woman, but he also knew how powerful deathbed promises could be. His own mother had made her father, his grandfather, promise to take Grey to New Mexico when she died. "Be a father to him..." Grey had never known his supposedly Irish father, who had run off before he was born.

Grey had only been six or seven when his mother passed, but he could still hold her face in his mind, and not even Armando teased him when he learned that Grey spoke with her as if she were still alive. He knew his mother's spirit had left this world, but he liked to imagine she was still here, watching over him, protecting him from harm.

Then it dawned on him...

Did Miss Carmen's mother have a vision about the Skinwalkers? Was this the "anything bad" she had warned her daughter against?

A shiver ran up Grey's spine, and it wasn't from the cold.

He was well over six feet tall now, so it wouldn't take much more effort to reach the ledge. With his feet planted firmly on a solid chunk of rock, Grey reached up to grab hold of another rock just beyond his fingertips. Dirt and dried roots slid down, and he averted his face before swallowing too much. He spat out most of it but didn't want to stop to rinse out his mouth.

He was glad the sun wasn't staring him in the eyes. The moon's light was gentle enough to guide his way. He tried another handhold to the left, and it held firm. He stepped up to another rock, then another, and realized there was a natural rhythm to climbing, as if his fingers had eyes.

His boots seemed to find just the right grooves as well. While Grey hadn't believed in signs and portents, he was beginning to, and this truth renewed his energy. With the ledge just a few feet above, Grey reached over and up, grabbing hold. He paused for a moment, making sure that it could hold his weight before clambering up.

Grey took a few moments to catch his breath, then peered over the ledge. He'd climbed a lot further than he'd thought. The ground loomed a few hundred feet below. Surprised by an unexpected wave of vertigo, Grey scrunched up his knees to rest his head. He closed his eyes, took a few deep breaths.

It was so quiet here. Not even the sound of a jackrabbit scurrying to its den or the scuttling of a spider. Peaceful. Yes, this place was peaceful. Whoever this woman was, Grey knew that she was a woman of power. She would know what to do.

Grey reached for his water skin, took a sip, spit it out over the edge, then took another and another until he'd washed out all the dirt, soothed his sore throat. He kept drinking until his thirst was quenched. For the first time since he'd left the de la Madrid ranch, Grey realized he wasn't crazy to come here. His thoughts turned to Armando and Miss Carmen, imagining them in each other's arms.

Grey took his pack off and leaned it against a rock. He'd been right. There was a recess behind the ledge, with plenty of room for him to stretch out and not worry about rolling off. He peered into the dark recess and realized he'd need his lantern to see more clearly. He opened a side pouch on his pack where he'd wrapped a small kerosene lamp. There was some flint in another pouch, which he struck against a rock, lighting the small mound of twigs he'd collected along the way. He had some others, which Miss Carmen had thoughtfully packed, and wondered how she knew so much about these things. She was a rare girl, Grey mused. No wonder Armando loved her.

A small blaze welled up when he lit the lantern. He hated the scent of kerosene, but it was better than an old-fashioned torch the wind could blow out.

Grey crouched down, holding the lantern in front of him to peer through the opening. It was more than just a slash in the mountain.

There was more than enough room for him to pass through. He held the lantern with one hand, as close as he dared, dragging his pack with the other, and was relieved that the rent opened into a larger area.

He took slow, cautious steps at first, then grew more confident as he passed through a narrow corridor into a small room with an alcove. This was no lair for coyotes or other beasts. Someone definitely lived here, as there were several containers and bed rolls, and there, glinting in the wan light, was a small figurine resting on a well-made shelf.

He stepped closer to the figurine, held the lantern above it. It was made of some type of smooth metal, but whoever made it was a true artisan. There wasn't a single hammer or file mark marring its surface. Grey peered even closer, watched as wisps of his cold breath surrounded the small statue like an early morning mist. Not even moisture beaded upon its surface.

He reached out to touch it, then pulled his hand back. What if it was an amulet? He reached out again, cautiously, this time just with his index finger, and jerked back when he felt a mild jolt.

Then he remembered the package Miss Carmen had given him. Grey set the lantern down on the hard-packed earth, sat down beside it, pulling his pack onto his lap. He un-cinched it, reached down beneath the protective layers of clothing for the package. It was wrapped in several layers of thick waxed paper, then again with burlap, and tied with twine.

"Promise me you won't open it," Miss Carmen had said so vehemently that just holding the package had made him nervous.

"I promise," Grey had replied, even more curious about the contents of this supposed gift.

Grey held the package for a moment longer, then stood up to place it next to the metal figurine. He sat back down, yawned. He thought about sleeping, but his mind was whirring with so many questions. Was he supposed to stand vigil for the woman or just wait until she appeared to him? He hadn't thought much further than this point.

His stomach rumbling, Grey reached into a pouch, pulled out one of the packets of food Miss Carmen had packed. Corn bread and beef jerky. There was cheese in another pouch, and he pulled that out, too, started to eat, taking his time, mulling over what he and Armando had seen that night near the woods.

They had looked like normal men and women, about nine or ten of them. It had been unusually dark, barely a sliver of a moon in the night sky. Their faces had been shrouded by brush and shadow. He and Armando had thought it was some of the ranch hands with their women, and had ventured closer to investigate, hoping to see... Well, just hoping to see what they were doing. Neither he nor Armando had ever been with a woman, and they were curious. Armando especially so, since now that Louis was gone, he had a real chance with Miss Carmen.

And then Louis stepped out from behind a tree. But how could that be, as what was left of him had been buried weeks before? One of the de la Madrid's ranch hands was there, too, and while Grey couldn't remember the man's name, he was certain it was him. But he was dead, too.

They'd covered their mouths to stifle their surprise, backed slowly away, afraid to make the smallest of sounds, when they both recognized a girl from school who always made moon eyes at them.

It was impossible! They were all dead. Were these spirits trapped on earth, unable to leave the place of their death?

The girl had disappeared shortly after Louis had, and there'd been some talk that the two of them had run off together because Louis never wanted to marry Miss Carmen. But then they'd found Louis, and a week later, Elena.

His grandfather had told him that some people could see spirits as if they were still flesh and blood. Were he and Armando both able to do that? No. Something else was going on here. Maybe they weren't dead after all. It was some hoax for the newspapers or a plot by some out-of-town developers to buy up land on the cheap.

That made more sense than anything else.

But what if he was thinking about it all wrong? Maybe there was some truth to the legends, and Louis and the others weren't even human. Could they have shed their winter skin like snakes in spring to reveal something else underneath? How had Louis's father even known it was his son? Elena's mother, her daughter? Just by the clothes, shoes, and other items scattered around their lifeless bodies.

Grey took another sip of water, ran a hand through his hair. *I must be a mess*, he thought, and hoped the woman wouldn't be offended by his appearance. He raked his hands through his long, black hair, tied it with a leather thong, then dribbled water on the corner of a cloth, wiped his face. It came away so dirty that he repeated the process until the day's filth was washed away. Then he washed his hands, rinsed out his mouth, and spit in a corner hidden by shadows.

Sleep. All he needed was some sleep, and in the morning, the woman would find him. And if she didn't, he would go in search of her.

He yawned, heard a click in his jaw, yawned again, and stretched out his limbs. His muscles weren't sore yet, but he was sure they would be in the morning. Grey unrolled his bedding, took off his boots, and was about to massage his feet, then realized that he was still hungry. He broke off another piece of cornbread and cheese. There was some dried fruit, too. Miss Carmen had thought of everything.

After he'd eaten, then drank more water, Grey stretched out on his bedroll. He wanted to keep the lantern on but didn't want to waste fuel. While he wasn't afraid of the dark, he was concerned about not being able to see more of his surroundings, as the shaft of moonlight piercing through the rent in the rock wall only provided a thin streak of light.

Even though Grey wasn't much for praying, he sent out a prayer of sorts in his mind, that the woman would come, that she would accept Miss Carmen's gift, then help them. He yawned again, sighed as he pulled the thick woven blankets around him. His last thought before drifting toward sleep was that if he could find a way to stop who, or what, it was from killing, he would be able to pay back Miss Carmen's family for taking him in after his grandfather died last fall.

And he would also be a man. What that meant for him, he wasn't sure of yet, but he knew that his life would have more direction if he could accomplish this task.

Grey rolled over, drifted to sleep, and into a dream where he was chased by faceless creatures calling after him in unknown tongues. He ran and ran until a strange golden wagon swooped down to hover just in front of him like a hummingbird, bathing him in silver light. And within that light was a face radiating like the moon. She was like no woman Grey had ever seen, and he backed away, less in fear than for wanting to see her more clearly.

She was tall, with a broad face and high cheekbones, and even though her hair was silver like an elder's, she was still young. Her limbs were long and slender but poised as if to gather and then release a power so fierce that he knew she must be a warrior.

But it was her pale, iridescent skin and those eyes shimmering like the inside of an abalone shell that drew him closer with unsuppressed awe.

He had never had such a dream, Grey realized upon waking. Was this a gift from his mother, a taste of the dreamtime his grandfather had once, and only once, spoken of? He rubbed the sleep from his eyes, fumbled around for his water skin, then froze, his hand perched above his mouth, water spilling down, soaking his shirt.

It hadn't been a dream. Not all of it, as there, standing before him, was the woman warrior from his dreams.

"My sister is dead, and you have come for my help," she said in his mind.

All Grey could do was nod.

The woman said to call her Lali. He wondered why Miss Carmen hadn't told him this woman was her *tia*, her aunt. Lali shared many things that he couldn't wrap his mind around, but it didn't take long for him to believe that anything was possible.

Even the legends.

Especially the legends.

As they prepared to leave for the de la Madrid ranch, Lali was wearing a fake skin like Carolina's mother had worn all those years, and if he hadn't seen her change before his eyes, he wouldn't have believed it was possible. One moment she was pale and lithe with silver hair, and the next, she was a bit heavier, with long, black hair and eyes to match. The device that controlled her shapeshifting was a thick silver band she wore around her wrist. It was inlaid with smooth, round stones that sparkled in the wan light.

After witnessing Lali's transformation, Grey didn't think their near-instantaneous trip to the ranch was all that strange. "I could get used to traveling without moving if I had a choice in the matter," he said to Lali as they walked around the thick clay wall surrounding Miss Carmen's house. Grey lifted the latch on the wrought iron gate and moved aside for Lali to go first. He could smell the herbs in Miss Carmen's kitchen garden, and he felt relieved to be home.

Esteban opened the back door before they even knocked. He and Carmen had been anxiously waiting for their return. So, too, had Armando, who grabbed and hugged him as if they were still boys.

"*Hola*, Lali," Esteban said, extending his arms. "So nice to see you again. You know then about *mi* Carolina. Your sister..."

"Yes. She will be missed, " she said, "but *now*, we must take care of these Skinwalkers, as you call them."

Some men from the de la Madrid ranch were in the kitchen, along with a few others he'd seen in town. Grey knew they wouldn't be here if they couldn't be trusted with stuff that was even weirder than what they'd already seen or heard.

While Lali and the others discussed plans, Grey took a few moments to fill in Armando, who kept shaking his head like he knew Grey had gone loco.

"It's true," Grey said. "That cave is a lookout station, and they have a ship that sails through the sky. It's docked beyond the clouds right now, beyond our atmosphere."

"You mean a sky ship," Armando whispered, "like the one that crashed. Are they from Mars or something?"

Grey shrugged. "I think she said they were from the Pleiades."

"You read too much, " Armando said, punching him in the arm.

"No, really. You'll see. Just ask Miss Carmen. She'll tell you."

"I already did," she replied, "but he won't believe me until he sees it for himself. You know how stubborn he can be." She smiled at Armando in the special way she reserved for him, and Grey chuckled when he saw his friend blush.

"Maybe she'll take us on her ship," Grey sighed, imagining the view of the valley, the ranches, how they would slip through the sky. But now, as he looked at Esteban and the men he'd gathered, armed with rifles and knives, ropes, and pickaxes, that possibility was almost as far away as the stars. They were planning to go up to the old gold and silver mine. It had been condemned and had been closed for nearly a year. Gas fumes or something.

Señor de la Madrid motioned his daughter and her friends over to the table, where a rough map was laid out.

"We have to find where they're nesting. I agree with Esteban." Lali nodded in his direction. "They wouldn't go deep into the mine, but they would definitely need somewhere to hide."

"But what if they'd moved on to another town? What then?" asked Mack, one of the ranch hands.

"Their skins wouldn't last that long," she said. " They would know this. They'll be looking for new ones soon, but without proper treatment, none of the skins will last longer than a week or two."

"There haven't been any new bodies—yet," Esteban offered.

"So, it's not a hoax," an older man shook his head. "Are they from that crash last year?"

Lali turned toward him, her dark eyes flashing even though her face appeared calm. "No, they have been here for a while. Lived in this valley and the one over the ridge. But what is important is that we capture and take them home, where they will be dealt with by *our* laws."

"I say we skin them alive ourselves—see how they like that!" a thin, wiry man yelled out, then collapsed on one of the kitchen chairs. Grey wondered whose father or husband he was.

"How do we stop them?" Miss Carmen asked, ending her silence.

"With this," Lali said, holding out another kind of contraption that looked like one of those fancy snuff boxes Grey had seen some of the traveling merchants use.

"But why do they take people's skins?" Armando asked, trying not to imagine the pain involved.

"These beings aren't like me or Lina, Carmen's mother. They don't look human. They're from another planet in our system, and we let them stay when many of us left. They'd grown used to life here, used to living as humans. We are to blame for not foreseeing this."

"But why did they change into... into..." Carmen couldn't seem to finish her thought, but what she meant was present in all their thoughts.

Grey reminded himself that she had been the one to take and hide her mother's false skin and the silver band that activated it. Her father, she had told them, was overcome with grief, had wanted to burn or bury it. Carmen had intervened in time.

Lali said, "They use a special tool to skin people. But since the skins they steal are not synthetic, they begin to decompose without treatment."

She held out another device to them. It looked like a simple metal pipe to Grey, but he could feel it pulse like a pitchfork struck by lightning.

"I've alerted our ships. We have the means to capture them, but I am concerned about your local authorities."

"You'd think that they would be grateful, especially the sheriff, but what if the Skinwalkers see us coming—or what if they try to capture *you*?"

"The local authorities won't bother us. They've recently lost a few deputies," Esteban interjected. "Very few people are going out at night, and if they do, it's in groups armed with shotguns and buck knives, which are no match for the device you mention." He sighed, rubbed a weary hand through hair that had gone almost completely white since his wife passed away.

"These are men whom I trust. The sheriff in Santa Fe is a corrupt man, a dishonorable man. He made a show of visiting all the ranches offering protection—but for a fee. No one has seen him lately."

"He's a coward," spat one of the men.

"Yeah, a coward. I hope those Skinwalkers got to him."

"We go tonight, then?" Esteban said.

Lali nodded. "A few hours before dawn would be best."

Just the thought of going up to the mines, especially in the dark, didn't sit well with Grey, but he could tell that it terrified Armando. His friend put on a good face, though, not wanting his Carmen to think he was less of a man. Knowing they weren't alone, plus having Lali's people in their sky-ships, helped a bit, but still... it was the mines.

Grey knew the Skinwalkers were dangerous. Even if they didn't want his skin, they could take it anyway as a diversion. If they got to him, to any of them, they would die in excruciating agony, their skin peeled meticulously from their body, leaving raw flesh in its wake. No one could survive such an ordeal—and wouldn't want to. Armando had already promised to slit his throat if that happened, and he had promised to do the same for his lifelong friend. Carmen, fortunately, had promised to stay with the other women and children in the ranch's cellar.

The mine stank worse than wet hay and pig excrement, worse than rotten eggs and kerosene, worse than anything Grey had ever smelled in his life. Lali placed a hand over his mouth, and the urge to retch disappeared. He nodded his thanks. What other powers did this woman of the Sky Clan have?

The group split up, with Esteban leading five men and Lali leading the other five plus him and Armando. There was a hum on the wind like bees or wasps swarming. Lali told him it was one of their ships waiting just beyond the ridge.

The Skinwalkers were toward the back of one of the side tunnels leading into a partially dug pit. Spanish, English, and some foreign—

no, *alien*—words carried toward Grey and the others as they inched along the tunnel sideways, their backs to the wall.

Did the Skinwalkers know they were being hunted? Their voices sounded serious but conversational. There were no obvious signs of their being riled.

At first, they thought there were eleven of them, but now it seemed there were fewer—unless there were others lying in wait.

Esteban's group was approaching the mine's other entrance. The map indicated that it was a safeguard, but Grey didn't know much about mines other than to avoid them. He'd heard stories of them collapsing, of men being buried alive or maimed. Then there were the fires that often came out of nowhere. Part nature, part careless-ness, part murderous intent.

Lali motioned that she was going on ahead. She had another device that looked like a thick playing card that helped her locate the Skinwalker's exact location. Grey had no idea how body heat could be measured, but Lali assured him it could.

With his heart pounding in his ears, Grey waited. They all waited for her safe return. Moments seemed like minutes, minutes, hours, and then she returned.

"They're just beyond that passage. There are only five of them. The others have died."

Grey resisted the urge to yelp with joy. They outnumbered the Skinwalkers!

And then Grey remembered the skinning tool. How many of them had one? He thought to ask Lali, then realized that all the creatures needed was one.

Lali motioned them to fan out, then sent Armando to tell Este-ban what she'd learned. Armando took off running.

Grey was careful where he stepped, afraid to send any chunks of rock scuttling across the ground. As they approached the tunnel, he could hear the Skinwalkers talking loudly. He knew sounds echoed and hoped that the Skinwalkers didn't have any special senses that would alert them to their commingled presence.

The further they walked into the mine, the more he wondered about Lali's people, how they could see through walls of rock to what was inside. For a moment, Grey wished that he was in their sky-ship watching these events unfold, then realized that he was glad to be here, proud to be able to help—despite his fear. What would his grandfather say? That courage was being afraid and still moving forward to do what needed to be done? He hoped that his grandfather and mother would be proud of him. He also hoped his grandfather knew he now *knew* the legends were true. Grey had a strong feeling that his grandfather had met the Sky People before. Perhaps he had even known one or more of them.

Was that why his mother made his grandfather promise to bring him here to Santa Fe?

The mine was sweltering, and Grey felt a wave of vertigo. He stopped to lean against the rough rock wall. Lali sent words of encouragement to him.

And then the stench intensified. One of the men fought back bile. Another retched on his boots.

Grey fingered the device in his pocket, his only weapon, mentally playing out what he was supposed to do. All of the men had one, as well as other weapons. Grey had never used a gun or a knife except for cutting food and other daily tasks. He had never taken a life, of an animal or a human, and he didn't want to have to take an alien's life unless it was absolutely necessary. The Skinwalkers couldn't be allowed out of this mine except as captives.

Or dead.

Just a few more steps and their bulbous heads came into view. Only two of them still had human faces, and of those two, only one had an intact skin. The others looked like they'd been flayed, with ribbons of flesh dangling from their backs and arms.

Just a few more steps and Grey saw that beneath the flayed skin was furrowed flesh, like a worm or grub. He imagined squishing them between his thumb and forefinger, willing it to be that easy.

Just a few more steps and Lali would give the signal for them to descend. He tilted his head to listen for Armando and the others.

They should have been here by now. He hoped that there weren't other Skinwalkers waiting to ambush them.

His heart pounded, and his throat was dry and scratchy from the heat and dust. They'd brought water, even some food, but no one felt the least bit of hunger. No one wanted to pause to drink.

When was the signal going to come? Grey intensified this thought, hoping that Lali would respond, but he heard nothing in his mind. She remained crouched down a few feet away, so still despite the awkward position.

The other men looked forward, too, barely breathing. Luke, who was about his age, was pressed against the wall as if willing himself to sink within its protective depths.

Then Lali rose to her full height, stepped away from them, and into the Skinwalkers' sight.

She spoke to them in an alien tongue, and from where Grey and the others waited, she sounded calm, like she was reasoning with them, offering them a way out without further violence. Or at least that had been the plan she told them. First, try this, and then if that doesn't work...

The Skinwalkers didn't seem surprised to see her. Grey thought he heard one of them laugh, an oddly human sound.

But it was clear they were angry.

Lali gave the signal. Grey and the others started forward, then halted as Esteban and his men ran toward the Skinwalkers, weapons drawn.

Grey wanted to move forward, but his feet wouldn't budge. It was as if they were embedded in stone. It was happening to the others, too, and he was certain it wasn't fear that froze them in place but another one of Lali's otherworldly devices.

A few moments later, the screaming began. Muffled at first, then with spine-tearing agony amid inhuman snarls. Someone was throwing rocks, shots rang out, and then Grey was finally able to move his feet. He ran forward, hoping that Armando was all right. That they would all survive.

The other men followed close behind. Grey fought for breath as his eyes scanned the scene. No nightmare could have prepared him for this...

The Skinwalkers had altered their form. Where their eyes should have been were long, narrow slits, their noses flat with nostrils flaring. From loose folds of skin, spikes like porcupine quills or cactus needles protruded. *How could these creatures ever appear human?* They'd lived among them. How?

One of the Skinwalkers moved forward, tearing at the last vestiges of its false humanity, wiping the bloody shreds of skin on its pants. It was grinning and looked right at Señor de la Madrid. Armando yelled out, "Noooooooooooooo!" and pushed Carmen's father out of the way just in time. Another man went down in his place, his skin peeled away and tossed aside amid a cacophony of breathless screams.

Grey lifted his arm, squeezed down on the device, pointed it directly at the Skinwalker who turned, snarling in his direction. Grey was afraid it hadn't worked and was going to press it again, but then the creature stopped in mid-stride, shuddered, as a nearly transparent fiber encased his body.

The others backed off, their arms extended in front of them. Lali motioned the men forward, and within minutes, the other Skinwalkers were imprisoned as well.

Over the next few days, Grey tried to find the right time, and the right words, to tell Armando he was leaving with Lali. After all that he'd seen, all that Lali had shown and shared with him, he couldn't imagine not going with her. She had known that he wanted this and smiled at his hesitation in asking. Finally, she had said it aloud for him.

"You want to go home, don't you?"

All Grey could do was nod, much like the first time he had met her.

But there was a price for leaving. He wouldn't be able to return for many years. The hardest thing was saying goodbye to Armando and the de la Madrid's, who had treated him as more than just a ranch hand. They had made him part of their family. Still, from the moment he had met Lali, he knew his path was with her and the people of the Sky Clan.

His grandfather would want this, his mother, too, as this was why they had come to Santa Fe. So he could return to his people.

He couldn't just leave without saying something to Armando, who was going to marry Miss Carmen in the summer. Esteban had given his blessing without hesitation; Armando had, after all, saved his life.

In the end, though, Grey had just said "goodnight," as if he was going to sleep, exhausted from the ordeal they had survived together. Just before dawn, when Armando went to wake him for breakfast, Grey's bed hadn't been slept in. Carmen peeked through the guest room door. Lali hadn't slept in her bed, either.

It was clear to them both where they had gone... To the stars and the home of the Sky Clan.

RED RAIN

Michael McCarty

**PART ONE:
RED SKIES AT NIGHT**

"At night, the black wings dry out
on the flat land.
At the end of the long road
comes the hand.
Slowly, the hand curls around the land
pinned with the wings..."

—Sheri Grutz

The rain was the color of blood, and the sky looked like it was bleeding. But we are not going to start here. We are going to start two weeks before that...

Chapter One

July 5th
11:00 p.m.

Everything that could go wrong went wrong for Mad Dawg. When he left Chicago to come back home for his sister's wedding in Park View, Iowa, he encountered extensive highway construction on Interstate 80. Normally, riding on his Harley Davidson Road King, he could make the trip in three hours, but because of roadwork, it took almost four hours. He parked his Hog in the church parking lot and barely got inside before they closed the doors to start the ceremony.

The wedding and the reception, of course, were a blast, seeing his little sister finally get hitched. At the banquet, the biker ate too much, drank way too much, and stepped into the bathroom too many times to hit the crack pipe.

His family and friends invited him to stay the night, but he would have none of that. Mad Dawg planned to get back on his Harley and head home. Being low on gas, he drove past the iron fence that spelled out the town's name and went to the PDQ convenience store.

Mad Dawg pulled the gas pump—it wouldn't start.

A voice came over the intercom, "After dark, it is per-pay inside or by credit card."

The biker walked inside and couldn't believe his eyes. At the counter was high school bully Brad Haskell, still big and tall, now with extra baggage around the waist, light blond hair with a bald spot, and a pencil-thin mustache that didn't really suit his face.

"I remember you from high school," Mad Dawg said.

Brad's eyes locked him. There was no recognition in his pale green eyes. "Is that cash or credit?"

"You used to beat the crap out of me every chance you got," the biker snapped. "I am now in a motorcycle gang in Chicago, and we beat the crap out of pencil pushers like you on a regular basis." He turned around, and on the back of his black leather jacket was the lettering "The Rattlers MC," with a drawing of a rattlesnake that was ready to strike.

"I don't want any trouble. Just pay for your gas and leave, okay?"

The biker stepped closer to the counter and reached his hand into his leather jacket.

"That was over five years ago. I really don't remember." The night clerk was trying to mask the fear in his voice but wasn't doing too good a job of it.

"Does your mama know how to sew?"

"Uh? What?"

"I said, does your mama know how to sew?"

"Yeah."

"Good. Have her sew this..." Mad Dawg quickly pulled out a switch-blade, opened the blade, and was prepared to slice the clerk's neck like a ham at Christmas dinner.

At that exact same time, the state trooper, Deputy Brandon Ruok, walked through the doors to get a refill on some coffee.

The biker became distracted. Instead of cutting the clerk's neck, he made a deep gash down the side of his face. Brad screamed his head off in pain. He was bleeding profusely; blood was all over his face and his shirt.

The policeman tackled Mad Dawg to the ground, cuffed him, and crammed him in the back of his police car. He never did get a refill on that coffee.

Before the biker was locked up in the Scott County Jail, he did get his one call. He managed to get a hold of a friend and fellow Rattler named Viper and told him everything that went down and asked the gang to come down to the Quad Cities to kick some major ass.

Chapter Two

July 6th
7:00 p.m.

Zoey Neumann drove past the fence with the giant letters that spelled out "PARK VIEW" on it and pulled into the PDQ parking lot. She got the wheelchair from the hatchback and helped her daughter, Sophie, onto it.

She pushed her daughter into the corner store, past the slushy machine and a refrigerator with shelves stocked with sodas, energy drinks, and beer.

Zoey needed to find something quick for dinner, and Sophie could sometimes be indecisive.

"Babe, what do you want for dinner?" she asked. They were next to the doors with the frozen pizzas.

Sophie pointed to the cheese pizza.

"Cheese? Don't you like anything else?" Zoey asked.

"Nope!" said Sophie.

"Okay, cheese pizza it is. For the second time this week."

Sophie giggled.

Zoey handed the frozen pizza to Sophie. They were in line behind three other people at the PDQ, waiting to pay for the pizza.

It had been ten years ago when her first husband, Leo, and Sophie were in an automobile accident. A drunk driver ran his truck through a red light, killing her husband and crippling her daughter. Sophie was only four years old then. Now that she was fourteen, it was hard to believe that it happened a decade ago. It still felt like yesterday. Losing her husband and her daughter losing the ability to ever walk almost devastated her, but she had to be strong for her child.

Zoey saw Dana "Pinky" Kincaid standing in the back of the line with a handful of energy drinks and a frozen pepperoni pizza. She used to babysit for Sophie years ago, but the young lady seemed lost in her thoughts. She didn't want to disturb her.

She was lost in her own thoughts about the past when her daughter yanked on her shirttail. "Hey, Mom, is that the Toxic Frankenstein?" Sophie asked.

Zoey turned her face so Sophie couldn't see her mouth opening wide in disbelief. She knew her daughter loved wrestling, and standing behind them in line was a huge man in a leather jacket with rhinestones on it that spelled out "TOXIC FRANKENSTEIN." He was six-foot-six and weighed over two hundred and fifty pounds. He was in his mid-fifties but obviously in great shape, like he worked out every day.

Zoey would feel like a failure of a parent if she lied to her own kid, but she knew it was him. Then, finally, she said, "I don't know, honey."

"I think it is him. Oh my God, I think it is him," Sophie said excitedly. She had a notebook with stickers of the wrestler plastered all over and was pointing to the Toxic Frankenstein one. Her daughter was wearing a red and black argyle sweater and a fluffy pink tutu with red-and-black-striped stockings underneath.

Zoey opened her purse and pretended to look for something, hoping the former wrestler hadn't heard Sophie's question.

The store employee, Josie Lamberson, was used to seeing them come in. She rang up the pizza. Zoey handed the cashier her credit card.

"Young lady..." The tall man with gray hair bent down so he wasn't towering over her. "...I used to be the Toxic Frankenstein. I'm now retired and living in my childhood home here in Park View. It is a simple life, but I'm happy."

Sophie was almost too stunned to respond.

"We really shouldn't be bothering the man," Zoey interjected. Something about this tall man just gave her the creeps.

"I understand. Stranger danger and don't talk to them and such. My name is Stan Bishop, and I own the farm across the road from

Park View Pentecostal Church, but you can call me Toxic Frankenstein, I don't mind. I started wrestling in high school, got a scholarship to wrestle at the University of Iowa, and then turned pro. The moral of it all is: Stay in school."

Zoey couldn't believe the positive school message she was hearing. But it made sense, as he probably made a lot of appearances and lectures at schools in his life.

"I was a professional wrestler for twenty years," he said with a dry laugh. "My fans are the cherry on top of my fudge sundae of life. Do you want my autograph?"

"Do I? Yes, I do!" Sophie said with much enthusiasm, but at the last moment, she remembered her manners. "Please? How much?"

"Oh, I don't charge. I'm too old for that." He gave her a wink. "Where do you want me to sign?" he asked.

Sophie handed him her notebook. "Anywhere inside."

The former wrestler signed his name and doodled a caricature of himself next to it.

Zoey was surprised at how nice the former wrestler was. She heard he was a gun nut with a small arsenal at his place and that he had turned his cellar into a bomb shelter. Other rumors said he was a zealous Bible thumper and a conspiracist who would spout crazy theories at the drop of a hat. He always talked about the end of the world or UFOs taking over the planet or that the world was going to be flooded again with the Great Flood like Noah had.

Zoey wanted to exit quickly, but her daughter was now intrigued by the wrestler, and he was being friendly enough to her.

All three stepped outside.

A teenage boy skateboarded near them, almost hitting Sophie. The teenager screamed, "Screw off, old man!"

"Nobody has respect for their elders these days," he sighed.

"Ain't that the truth," Zoey said.

"I think it is going to rain, Mama," Sophie stated.

"I reckon it might," he said, looking at the dark clouds.

"Tonight's rain isn't going to be too bad," Sophie continued. "But in a couple of days, it is going to be bad. Real bad."

Zoey looked to the sky and scanned the clouds above. It could rain; it might not. That's how Iowa's weather was. "Sophie is always good at predicting the weather. Maybe she'll become a meteorologist," she said with a nervous laugh.

"You can't control the weather," he said. "The weather controls you. Good day, ma'am and young lady."

Zoey nodded. "Goodbye, Mister Bishop."

He nodded and walked over to his Dodge Ram truck.

"That's funny. There isn't any rain in the forecast for this week," Zoey responded, unlocking the car doors. She was used to this; she helped her daughter get in the seat and put the wheelchair in the hatchback. Sophie was a living barometer. So many times, there was no rain in the forecast, but Sophie would say it was about to rain, and sure enough, it rained. Maybe the accident brought this ability out in her.

On the way home, Sophie was fixated on the sky through the passenger window. Zoey hoped it wouldn't be a storm, as Sophie didn't like the blast of the severe weather siren warnings.

Once they arrived home, Zoey turned the oven on to 425° to preheat.

Sophie rolled her wheelchair to the front window and began her storm watch.

Zoey noticed that her husband, Mark, had left his cell phone on the kitchen table. She picked it up and saw the notification of a text message from Sarah, his boss. She knew his passcode, so she unlocked his phone and looked at his messages with Sarah. "Stay late tonight, Mark-baby. I bought a new bra and panties from Victoria's Secret, and I'm dying to show you."

Scrolling back, she could see that they had been meeting secretly for months when he was supposed to be working late. There were several photos of his boss posing provocatively in her underwear. She almost dropped the phone.

Zoey suspected something was going on and that he might be cheating on her, but this was the proof she needed.

She started thinking about a way to get back at him. She had a wicked idea, but it could possibly cost her her job, even land her in prison—if she got caught, so she had to make sure she wouldn't get caught.

Chapter Three

July 10ᵗʰ
5:25 p.m.

Strange lights were seen hovering in the placid blue sky of Park View, Iowa, just north of Davenport and south of Clinton.

It was a hot, humid, and hazy dusk as Zach Zobeck, a.k.a. Z.Z., stepped off the back porch into the yard. Tall and lean with dark hair and hazel eyes, along with a handlebar mustache that looked a bit out of place on his babyface, the 21-year-old college dropout was now living with his Uncle Ed, who everyone just called Greybeard because of his long, gray ZZ Top beard.

Z.Z. was not used to the backbreaking farm life of hauling heavy bales of hay, bending in any number of positions to work on different agricultural equipment, or cleaning the horse stalls, but it beat working some low-paying job in the Quad-Cities or flunking out of St. Ambrose University again; that would be a nightmare.

"Bix!" he yelled.

No response.

That was typical of his overweight brown Beagle named after a dead jazz musician from Davenport, Iowa.

He was about to yell for his dog again when something strange and moving amazingly fast in the sky caught his eye. It wasn't a bird or a kite—it was much bigger than that. Not a plane or a helicopter. It was weird and different and a little frightening. The cornflower-blue sky was being invaded with hunter-green mammatus clouds that had a fluorescent glow to them.

Suddenly, a metallic trilling warbling sound could be heard from overhead. It sounded like a flock of hummingbirds flying close by, but there were only glowing clouds floating on the skyline.

A strong gust of wind almost knocked him over; if the barndoor had not been against his back, he would have been on the ground.

"Bix!" he yelled even louder.

This time his dog came running out of the barn to his master's feet.

Zach peered into the sky once more. He wasn't sure if a storm was brewing or if something else was coming.

Dusk was creeping in; the summer sky was still bright, but that's how summers were. A shooting star crossed the sky, but it was too early for stars to appear; it was a meteorite with a tail of bright red flames high in the sky. It zoomed across the horizon and crashed behind the barn.

Z.Z. ran behind the barn to the marsh where the fireball crashed.

He stood on the edge of the muddy bog and Bix barked bravely behind him. He looked down at the eerie crimson glow; it lasted for a few moments, then turned black like the night.

"That's freaking weird," he said to his dog. "Freaking weird."

The beagle whined.

He looked up at the strange-looking clouds. "Let's go inside before it rains."

Chapter Four

July 10^{*th*}
5:29 p.m.

McKenzie Pham flipped her flowing, shiny, black hair over her bare right shoulder and slowly started to gather her things. She was wearing a blue top with spaghetti straps, a skirt that barely covered her knees, and sandals. She grabbed the cell phone from her purse and turned off the airplane mode. Her dark eyes squinted, then widened and rolled when she saw there were seven missed calls from Doug Casadidio.

She sat, pensive, and waited for the aisle to clear of those who were eager to get off the plane. She certainly wasn't in any hurry. She took her time gathering her brown leather carry-on bag from the overhead compartment.

"Seven frigging calls," she muttered to herself as she slung the carry-on bag over her right shoulder and adjusted her small black purse to her front. Who calls someone seven times in a row like that?

She slowly walked down the aisle of the plane and instinctively smiled at the flight attendant as she exited the plane and started down the blue felt walkway that led into Moline International Airport.

She had just spent two months interning at an Indiana veterinary clinic. They loved her and asked if she could return next summer. She had taken the first steps towards her veterinary career. Eight more years and she would be there.

McKenzie was growing weary of her high school sweetheart, Doug. His aspirations were all about the World of Warcraft and Grand Theft Auto. These days, they really didn't seem to have anything in common. She had earnest life goals. He had high game-score goals.

"McKenzie!!" he yelled across the airport. He ran over and embraced her.

Chapter Five

July 10th
5:39 p.m.

The job was supposed to be simple enough, transporting a prisoner to Anamosa State Penitentiary from Scott County Jail. The driver, Joey Clemens, had done plenty of prisoner transfers. He was a retired policeman on the force for thirty years and now would do these jobs to supplement his pension. Also riding along was Ashton "Big Mac" McDonnell. This was his first time doing a job like this. At 6' tall and over 300 pounds, he wasn't too afraid. The big, bearded guy smirked while he held the loaded shotgun in the passenger seat.

Sitting in the back of the Scott County Jail prisoner transport van was the prisoner, twenty-eight-year-old Travis "The Panorama

Park Butcher" Krall. He was completely bald, wearing a bright-orange jumpsuit and humming the song "Riders of the Storm" by The Doors. His hands were handcuffed together on his lap, and his feet were cuffed to a metal bar on the floor.

Krall was found guilty of double first-degree murder and breaking-and-entering; he had broken into Rick and Connie Mason's house when the couple at night. Connie was taking a bath, and Rick was watching television. Mr. Mason was stabbed forty-four times. Connie ran out of the tub naked. The intruder pushed her to floor and raped her, then stabbed her twenty times with the same butcher knife. After that, he just walked down the street with the bloody knife in his hand. The police arrested him.

The van had just passed the Eldridge exit when Joey became very pale and sweat broke across his face; his breathing became heavy, laborious.

"Are you all right, man," Big Mac asked, concerned about the driver.

"Yeah," was the last thing the driver said before he had his heart attack.

The other guard had to unbuckle the seatbelt to go over to the steering wheel. By the time he unbuckled it, it was too late—the van slammed through the guardrail, down a small hill, and crashed into a big oak tree. He was thrown through the windshield and killed. The driver was also dead.

The impact into the tree ripped the car into two. The cage separating the back from the front was now broken wide open. Travis tried to rise, but his feet were still cuffed to the metal bar. Without the cage blocking the front and back, the prisoner reached forward and tried to grab the keys out of the ignition; he was too far back and could only brush them with his fingertips. He lunged as far as his shackles would allow, but his ribs began to ache. They didn't feel broken, maybe bruised, but they still hurt like hell.

Travis continued to press forward with all his might, which caused the cuffs around his feet to cut into his flesh and bleed. He was sweating profusely and blood began to pour around his feet. He pushed forward with all his strength once again; his face twisted with pain, and he screamed in agony the whole time, but in the end, it was worth it when he grabbed the keys out of the ignition, found the handcuff keys, and unlocked his feet and hands.

The prisoner crawled out of the back of the van.

Big Mac lay on the ground on the other side of the tree, he was covered in blood. it. He figured the OnStar had already notified the authorities, so he had to get out of there as soon as possible. He walked as fast as he could, limping on his left foot, which was the most cut up from the cuffs. It looked like it was going to rain soon; he had to find some shelter.

Chapter Six

July 10th
5:42 p.m.

The brown rusted 1999 Mercury Grand Marquis Station Wagon came to a complete stop against the curb. The driver, Uncle Brew, a dead ringer for Jimmy Buffet's fatter cousin, wore a gray suit jacket with a red, white, and blue T-shirt underneath that said "Red, White & Brew. I make beer disappear. What's your superpower?" He also had on baggy khaki pants, psychedelic flip-flops, and dark dollar-store sunglasses.

The overweight comedian celebrated his fiftieth birthday last week when a waitress gave him a cupcake with a candle on it.

His traveling companion was a big guy, too, looking like a forty-something Hispanic overweight Johnny Cash. He was dressed all in black with a matching cowboy hat. The magician was named *El Mago*, which was Spanish for "The Magician."

El Mago took out his earbuds and said, "What's up?"

"The two scariest words of summer—swampy underwear," Brew said. "It is an everglade in my shorts right now."

"T.M.I.," the magician smiled. "Are you giving me a weather report or testing new material on me?"

"Neither, just lost."

"Lost?"

"Stranded... In Iowa," the overweight comedian sang the last part, loud and out of tune.

"I don't get it."

"It's an old song by Manfred Mann's Earth Boy Band, or maybe it was Chumbawamba—I don't remember."

"We're in Iowa? I thought we were still in Illinois."

"You slept when we crossed into the Hawkeye State."

"What city are we in?"

"Park View."

"How did you know that?"

"Because we're parked in front of a sign that says, 'Welcome to Park View, Iowa.'" He paused. "Across the street is a church that also says Park View."

"Park View? I never heard of it. Are we in the Quad Cities?"

"Don't know. Maybe." Brew opened his glove compartment, took out a rag, opened the car door, and stepped outside. He used the cloth to attack the crud, grime, and dead bugs on the windshield. "The last two-hundred miles, the air conditioner has been working badly. So has the windshield cleaner. After our next gig, I'll get both fixed."

"Good idea. Hey, did I ever tell you about the Comedy Hut?"

"No. I like that place. They have all those tikis and bamboo walls. It's a chain. Which one? Honolulu, LA, or Chicago?"

"There is one more in Kokomo."

"Like the Beach Boys song?"

"Yup."

Brew scratched his head and thought about it for a moment. "I remember that place now. I played it a few times early in my career."

"They sure remember you."

"Really?"

"You did a Tarzan impression and jumped up and grabbed one of the chandeliers, but it couldn't hold you and it came crashing down. Nobody was hurt, and the comedy club's insurance paid for it."

Brew laughed. "Youth. Brings back some good memories."

"Anyway, throughout the club, they have portraits of different comedians—George Carlin, Judy Tenuta, Richard Pryor—"

"All dead. But loved them all."

"I have a point to make."

"Okay, okay. Go on."

"Eddie Murphy, Steve Martin, Jeff Altman, Jay Leno—"

"Remember when you and I had seats on the first row of the balcony at the Ha-Ha House in St. Louis? We were throwing Doritos down on the stage during the middle of Jay's act. He looked up at us first. He was ticked, and then he realized what we were doing and said, 'Now that's funny.' Jay was doing commercials for Doritos at the time."

"Yes, I remember. Can I go on?"

"Please do."

"Anyway, they have those giant portraits gracing the walls of the club. And on the women's bathroom door is a portrait of comedienne Tammy Pescatelli. And on the men's bathroom door is yours."

This caused Brew to laugh so hard that he knocked over an open bottle of Mountain Dew, which spilled all over the floor. "That is funny," he said. "The comedy business has been pissing on me for years."

They were both silent for a moment, and Brew began singing "Raindrops Keep Falling on My Head."

Mago nodded. "Talking about raindrops, I've been hearing weird shit on Sirius, red rain across the country."

The comedian leaned next to the side of the car that had a magnetic sign displaying a drawing of two overweight cats—one was standing up hitchhiking, the other sitting on a suitcase with the words: "Two Fat Cats Comedy & Magic Tour."

The comedian looked to the sky, saw dark, maroon-colored clouds overhead, and decided to get back inside the vehicle. "The G.P.S. isn't working. Not sure how to get back onto Highway Sixty-one. Is Brady Street the same as Highway Sixty-one?"

Mago just shrugged. "Maybe you can ask that Padre across the street."

Brew turned his head. Sure enough, there was a man of the cloth standing on the shadowy porch in front of an old schoolhouse that had been turned into a church. It looked more like a one-room building with a large classroom than a place of worship. There was a bell tower with a big white cross on top and a faded sign that read "Park View Pentecostal Church."

The tall, old African American man with gray hair had a black patch over his right eye. He waved and walked off the steps toward the station wagon. "Jesus said to shake the dust off your feet," the man yelled. "Why don't you come inside before the storm? It looks like it's going to be a bad one."

Brew looked at the magician and just shrugged again. "Okay, let me pull this beast over to the other side of the road."

"I don't like the look of those clouds up there." The magician pointed to the dark, reddish storm clouds floating in the sky above.

"Yeah, they do look menacing," Uncle Brew said. "Possibly tornado weather."

"Do you know the other name for tornadoes?"

"Twisters."

"Yeah. I was thinking of another one."

Uncle Brew shrugged. "I give up."

"The Finger of God. Because nobody knows the path the tornado will take except the Lord above."

The comedian thought about it for a moment. "God has given me the finger plenty of times. Let's get going."

Chapter Seven

July 10th
5:52 p.m.

Josie Lamberson leaned forward on the counter at the PDQ, causing her short skirt to hike up just a little further. Four decades on this planet was starting to catch up to the assistant night clerk. Her blonde hair had to be dyed every other month, and the hazel eyes had lost their sparkle. Her body was still in pretty good shape despite all she had been through. Gravity wasn't of her friend as her Victoria's Secret push-up bra was getting a good working out.

Josie's love life, however, wasn't in that good of shape—too many marriages, too many divorces, and too many lovers in between.

Yet she leaned even further across the counter, causing the already short skirt to rise higher.

She knew the two in-store video cameras were pointed at the front door and the cash drawer; they wouldn't capture her skirt rising steadily upward. Nor would it detect Brad Haskell's enormous erection and the fact his eyes were practically bulging out of his skull.

Josie knew she was getting him all hot and bothered but didn't really care. Too many marriages, too many lovers. Her love life was wearing her out faster than her life was.

Brad fell into her type—big and stupid and after a few times making the box springs squeak, he would disappear, although he was a co-worker.

She sighed.

He wasn't much of a looker now, what with the side of his face bandaged.

A co-worker trying to look up her skirt was the least of her problems.

"Why did the guy cut you up again?" she asked the bandaged co-worker.

"Huh, what?" Brad took his eyes off her bottom and looked directly into her eyes. "He was some psycho greaser I went to high school with. If it wasn't for that cop, he probably would have carved the rest of my face up like a Jack-O-Lantern."

Just then, Brandon Ruok, the policeman who had saved Brad from being sliced up like a turkey on Thanksgiving, walked into the store. "Hey, Josie," he said, approaching the counter. "Hi, Brad."

Brad walked around the counter by the peace officer. "Thanks again, man," he said. "If you didn't stop that frigging lunatic, he'd cut the rest of my face off."

"Just part of the job," the lawman said as he refilled his coffee.

"Let me pay for it," Brad said. "It is the least I could do."

"Thanks."

Josie rang up the refill, and the younger man paid for it.

"I heard you were originally a police officer in Texas."

"Yup," the officer said, sipping his steaming hot coffee. "San Antonio."

"That biker was really stupid or really high."

"Well, the stupidity is hard to separate from alcohol or drugs. Unfortunately, when you get somebody with the intelligence and temperament of your average grizzly bear drunk, you're bound to wind up with a murder before the weekend's over. I believe that biker was both high and stupid," the officer said.

"So why did you move from Texas to Iowa?" the clerk asked.

"It is a long story. But mostly tired of the murders. Too many down there. Although it's starting to get really bad in Davenport."

The officer stirred his coffee and then continued. "Overall, we average between one-hundred-and-seventy-five and two-hundred homicides a year in San Antonio. That number goes up to around three hundred or so if you count intoxication-related car crash fatalities known in Texas under the criminal title Intoxication Manslaughter, which is one of the four classifications of murder in Texas."

"Moonshine involved?" Brad asked.

The police officer sighed. "I think, though, that alcohol is a factor in at least half of our homicides overall. That means the suspect, or the victim, or both are intoxicated at the time of the incident. It may not be the sole cause of the murder, but it is a significant factor.

"I haven't seen the breakdown yet for this year, but usually about sixty percent of our murders are gang- and/or drug-related. That number is almost certainly higher, but you see, the Mexican Mafia, our best customers, are fond of dropping off their handy work just over the county line in Atascosa or Medina County. Because the body gets found in some rancher's field in one of those counties, they must investigate the murder, even though we all know the crime itself probably took place in San Antonio. Jurisdiction issues are a thorny topic in my line of work."

Josie and Brad both looked at each other with surprise.

The officer took a sip of his coffee and continued. "Of the remaining forty percent of our murders, most are alcohol-related to some degree or another. You get the occasional genuine whodunit, but despite what prime time T.V. would lead us to believe, those kinds of murders are a statistically insignificant fraction of the overall homicide picture."

"So why did you move to Iowa again?" Josie asked, confused.

"I was a police officer in Texas for a decade. When you deal with that much violence, that much death, you start to think, maybe I should go someplace without a daily shooting. I have a cousin in this area, and I heard they were looking for officers," he said. "My break is almost up. I gotta go."

The officer walked out the doors, stepped out from under the awning, and looked up at the dark, red skies, it looked like it was going to rain soon.

Chapter Eight

July 10th
5:56 p.m.

Zoey Neumann drove the 2015 silver-gray Subaru Forester into the garage. Sophie was watching some Disney flick on her phone.

She pushed the garage door opener to close the door, but it wouldn't budge. She was close to swearing, but Sophie was sitting in the front seat. Just another "honey-do" thing her husband, Mark, hadn't gotten to.

After getting her daughter into the wheelchair and into the house, she emptied the cans of soup into the slow cooker before taking Sophie to school. Her husband didn't like canned soup, but when it stewed all day, he thought it was made from scratch. Homemade soup would have to wait, between working at the zoo, dropping Sophie off at school, and then picking her up, as well as keeping the house clean and doing laundry.

"Babe, do you want to watch T.V. for a bit? I'm going to change into some P.J.s."

"What about dad?"

"He's working late tonight. It'll be just us two again."

"Okay."

Zoey went upstairs, changed into silky, light-blue pajamas, and then came back downstairs. She was headed to the kitchen when she passed by the security monitors in the hallway and saw a man in an orange jumpsuit creeping by the gazebo near the back of their home. She looked at the monitors more closely and recognized Travis "The Butcher" Krall, the guy from the recent murder trial. She snatched her cell phone, but it was dead. She reached for the landline, and it, too, was dead. She tried to remain calm, realizing he couldn't break in because all the doors and windows were locked. Then she remembered the garage door was wide open. That is when she began to panic. A million thoughts raced through her mind. She had to protect her daughter at all costs; she had to protect herself as well. If she went upstairs to get her husband's gun, she'd be too far away from Sophie. If they went out the side door, there was no light in the backyard.

She opened the closet door and picked up a wooden bat. Her husband played baseball during the summer; it would make an adequate weapon.

"Sophie," Zoey whispered. "Come here, babe." She was afraid her daughter wouldn't hear over the TV, but she did.

She wheeled the wheelchair to her mother. "Go into the bathroom, lock the door, and don't come out until mom says so. Okay?"

"Okay," she said softly before wheeling into the bathroom and shutting the door.

She walked back to the security monitors; the intruder was in the garage with his hand on the door.

The Butcher opened the door, and when he saw Zoey, his face looked like a starving guy walking into an all-you-can-eat buffet. "I picked the right house," he said with a salacious smile.

Zoey slowly retreated toward the stairs, one step at a time.

"Don't get any funny ideas," she said, trying to sound tough but failing to do so.

"Funny ideas?" Travis said. "Like ripping these silk P.J.s off your body. That doesn't seem very funny, does it?"

"Get out!" she screamed.

He refused to move.

"Get out now!"

"No, I am going to get *in*," The Butcher said, pointing to her crotch. "Deep inside."

She took a swing at him with the wooden bat.

"Hey, batter, batter—swing," he said. "You can do better than that. I'm not a baseball; I'm much bigger than that."

"My husband will be home soon," she said.

"I killed before; I'm not afraid to kill again."

"I'm warning you," she said, swinging the bat again. "Leave. Now!"

He didn't say anything this time but kept looking between her legs and drooling like a wild animal; that's when he took a couple of quick steps in her direction.

This time, she swung with all her strength, the bat hitting him right in the middle of his chest. He grunted in pain as he fell backward, his head slamming against the wooden floor with a loud *thud*.

She studied him for a moment. Blood was all over his head and face, he didn't move, and his eyes were shut. She hurried down the stairs, holding the bat tightly in case he tried anything again. She nudged him with her foot. He still didn't move.

Zoey noticed that half of his body was lying on an area rug. "Sophie, come out. It's okay," she yelled. Her daughter opened the bathroom door, wheeled over to her mom, and hugged her.

She lugged Travis Krall on the area rug, he was heavy, and she was sweating profusely as she dragged him towards the garage. She only got a few feet; her back was killing her and so was her shoulders. She wanted to drag him outside, but she knew she couldn't get him that far. She also knew Sophie couldn't help either.

She stopped for a moment, took another breath, and then dragged the dead weight of the unconscious man to the nearby bathroom and left him lying on the floor, quickly shutting the door. The bathroom door didn't have an outside lock, only an inside one. She was going to grab the bat to use as some kind of leverage lock against the door, but she didn't want to be without a weapon either.

Zoey opened the inside door leading to the garage; normally, when the lights were out, it would be cave-like darkness, but because the garage door was stuck, there was some light inside. She was exhausted. The adrenaline rush had passed, and she waited to catch her breath again.

She heard some moaning coming from the bathroom, it was Travis. She had hoped that might have killed him, but he was very much alive.

Chapter Nine

July 10th
6:01 p.m.

After McKenzie grabbed her beat-up pink suitcase from the baggage carousel, she followed Doug to the parking lot and got into his father's F-150 pickup truck. As he drove out of the parking lot, he turned on the MP3 player. Some loud rap music with a vibrating bass-line blasted through the speakers.

"Can you turn down the music? I want to talk," McKenzie said.

"Yeah," he said, lowering the volume.

"Why is there a tire iron on the floor?" she asked.

"I had to change a tire yesterday, forgot to put it away."

"Okay. Tomorrow, do you want to go to the Ice Cream Palace with me?"

"It closed."

"What?"

"Yeah, at the end of last summer, shortly after you went to Ames. Didn't I tell you that?"

"No. I would have remembered that."

There was an awkward silence as the truck crossed the I-74 Bridge. McKenzie broke the silence. "Why did you cut the dreads?"

He didn't answer for a moment. "My lawyer told me to."

"What lawyer? Why?"

"You know Big Bird?"

Big Bird was the nickname for Barry Byrd, a tall teenage boy who was always in trouble with the law. All the police officers in Scott County knew the heavily tattooed kid by sight because of his tats and purple mohawk.

"We were at the P.D.Q. last March, and this Bozo driving a Party Wagon pulls up to the gas pumps and runs inside, leaving the keys in the ignition–"

"Party Wagon?"

"SUV—so you can get your boys some booze and some bud. Bird jumped inside, and so did I. We made it to Camanche before we were busted."

Stunned McKenzie, all she could say was, "Jesus."

He didn't say anything for a few moments, gripping the steering wheel tighter. "I ended up with two years' probation, worse for Bird. They gave him a dime."

She didn't say anything but gave a puzzled look.

"Ten years at Anamosa."

More awkward silence. She was tempted to say something about playing too many games of *Grand Theft Auto* but decided against it.

"It gets worse. Because of probation, I am required to have a job. My friend, Brad Haskell, was going to get me hired at the P.D.Q. But with the record now, they won't hire me. I guess I am going to have to detassel corn, which is still better than going to jail."

McKenzie was so aggravated she didn't realize they had already driven back to Park View and were at Scott County Park. Doug had stopped the truck on the side of the road and parked across from a picnic shelter. They had made out here plenty of times in high school.

Doug nuzzled her neck; she could feel his warm breath. He slid his hand down and started squeezing her right breast.

"I want to go home," she said.

He ignored her.

"I said I want to go home. NOW!"

Doug kept squeezing her chest.

She slapped his face, opened the door, and ran out of the truck.

"What the fuck, McKenzie? I haven't seen you in about four months and you do this shit?"

She felt something strike against the back of her neck. More and more of the substance descended from the fading twilight. It was raindrops, leaving crimson splotches on her white blouse.

It was the beginning of the red rain.

PART TWO:
RED RAIN

Chapter Ten

July 10th
6:00 p.m.

The alien bacteria had floated in outer space for hundreds of years. When it reached Earth, it reacted with its atmosphere, turning it into rain. Not Earth rain, but Earth rain mixed with alien bacteria, which turned it red. When a drop touched human flesh, it would eat away at it.

It rained all over the United States, all over the whole world.

It started with a few red drops falling here and there... And then it came down like a monsoon. Picture the ending of the movie *Carrie*, but instead of pig's blood falling briefly from the ceiling, it went on and on endlessly.

It was the top of the seventh inning, and the game was tied. The Park View Pelicans and the Clinton Lumber-Kings had three runs each. It was a sold-out game.

Patrick Stevenson, one of the umpires walked over to follow umpire Mitch Schmidt.

Patrick pointed to the sky. "I don't like those dark red clouds at all, man. Looks like it could be a tornado or something."

Mitch stared at the clouds for a moment. "Neither do I."

Agnes Jarett sat at the end of the gift-laden table. Her family, including her kids, grandkids, and even great-grandkids, neighbors, friends, and members of her church, had gathered to celebrate her one-hundredth birthday. Even a photographer from the *Quad-Cities Times* was there to take a photo of her when the cake was brought out and the candles lit.

Agnes's oldest daughter, Rose, looked up at the dark crimson clouds that suddenly appeared. "I hope it doesn't rain on Mom's one-hundredth birthday."

Allie Campbell lay on the blanket. She wore a black bikini that accentuated her curves in all the right ways. She had spent all morning dying her hair the right shade of bubblegum pink, but her boyfriend hardly noticed; he just stared salaciously at her swimsuit.

Her boyfriend, Johnny Everson, came out of the house holding two bottles. He was wearing red swim trunks that he was starting to outgrow. "I snagged some wine coolers out of my parents' basement fridge," he said, handing one to Allie.

They started dating in tenth grade at North Scott High. Now, tenth grade had ended, and they were about to take it to the next stage.

Everything was working out just great. His parents installed a privacy fence in the backyard a few weeks ago, and they were at the Pelicans and Giants baseball game at the park. The game would probably be over in about twenty minutes or so. After the game they'd head off to the local drinking establishment, Large Marge's, for a few hours.

"Now you have to live up to your end and take off your top for me," the high schooler said.

"I don't like the looks of those clouds. Maybe we should go inside."

"Naw, I want to see them in the daylight..."

Chapter Eleven

July 10ᵗʰ
6:04 p.m.

The three bikers guided their motorcycles into the dilapidated red barn at the Baumann's place. Each gang member wore a greasy black leather jacket illustrated with a rattlesnake ready to strike and emblazoned with the words "The Rattlers MC" underneath.

Grizzly pulled off his helmet and tossed it onto the wooden floor. He had long, dishwater-blond hair and a long, blond beard streaked with gray. He was a big guy, tall and heavy; his eyes were the color of melted chocolate but were unfriendly and unkind. He was wearing a black Harley Davidson T-shirt and torn jeans. He dismounted and walked to the door as the rain began to fall.

His girlfriend, Honey, slid off the motorcycle and put her helmet on the handlebars. She had a pageboy haircut; her honeysuckle dark blonde and light brown hair had long bangs that almost covered her cobalt-blue eyes. She was wearing a white, off-the-shoulder crop-top and torn jeans. Petite, not even five feet tall, she walked over to stand next to her very tall boyfriend.

Viper, the last Rattler to get off his bike, took off his helmet and put it on the seat. He had long dark hair almost to his shoulders. He was wearing a white wife-beater shirt and torn jeans. Most ladies either feared him or found him sexy in a bad-boy way, which was the way he liked it. He didn't smile but had an arrogant smirk on his long face. His criminal record was as long as the trip from Chicago to Park View. He stepped over his vehicle and joined his riding companions. The inside of the barn was dark, so he kept his headlight on. He knew he couldn't keep the headlight on forever or it would run down his battery. He scoped out the old barn; it looked like it was lucky to still be standing—old wood, rotten in many places, eaten by termites in others. Hay was scattered all over the place. There was a pitchfork leaning against the wall, and above that, a rusty old lantern on top of a wooden barrel next to where Honey parked her bike. He opened the lantern, took out the lighter he used for his crack pipe, and lit the wick. It illuminated the barn. He turned off his motorcycle headlight.

Viper looked out at the falling rain from the sky. "It's raining."

"No shit," Grizzly said.

"It's a strange rain. Red rain," Honey said. "I never seen anything like it before. It looked like someone stabbed God and He's bleeding from above."

"That's a creepy thought," Grizzly responded.

All three stood watching the red rain pour down.

"What do you think it is?" Honey asked.

"Don't know and don't want to find out," Viper said.

"Me neither," Grizzly said.

For a moment, the only sound was the falling rain.

"Do you wanna get high?" Grizzly asked.

"Not tonight," Honey said. "I've got a splitting headache because of the ride."

"What about you? Do you wanna get high?"

"Does a bear shit in the woods?" Viper asked.

"Hey, I'm a bear," he answered back.

"I've seen you shit in the woods, too," he replied with a laugh.

"Hey," Honey said, looking at her phone. "Are you guys getting any reception?"

"No."

Bear shook his head. "We're out in the sticks, and it's raining. We probably won't get service for hours."

"You're probably right." She walked to the other end of the barn, closer to the lantern.

Chapter Twelve

July 10th
6:07 p.m.

Greybeard was in his early sixties, and he lived up to his nickname with his bushy gray beard and gray hair. He sat in his oversized recliner with a can of Bud in one hand and the remote control in the other. He pointed the remote at the seven-foot flat screen, which was getting only snowy reception. He flipped from channel to channel with the same results.

"The overpriced Satellite pigs keep squealing for more money every month, and they give you dross service like this. I'm going to miss the Cubs playing the Cardinals," he said, finishing the can of beer. He tossed the empty into a box in the corner; it ricocheted off the wall and back into the container. "You're old enough to drink?"

Zach nodded his head.

"Grab a cold one for me and yourself. I wanna chat with you a bit."

The nephew opened the refrigerator, grabbed a couple of cans of Bud, and returned to the living room, giving his uncle one can and keeping the other for himself. His cousin, Lizard, was sacked out on the loveseat, snoring like a dull bench saw.

The uncle brushed a strand of his totally gray hair from his work uniform, a light gray jumpsuit that had a dead bug logo with the words "Big Bob's Bug Busters... The Bug Stops Here." The slogan was a pun on the buck stops here, which most people have forgotten over the years.

"How was work today?" Z.Z. asked, popping the tab on the beer.

"It was a real cooker outside, temps in the low nineties, hotter than a hot tub in Hades."

The young man laughed.

The older man continued. "A real bad cockroach job in East Moline, an okay bedbug reinspection in Clinton, and a real shitty raccoon job in Le Claire. The beast was living in the chimney. Z.Z., I'll tell you something about coons. They are a royal pain in the ass. Major pain. If you grab, say, Bix by the back of his neck, he will have a hard time moving his head around. Not those critters. If you're holding him by the scruff of his neck, he'll twist inside his skin and turn around and bite your hand lightning quick."

"Did the raccoon bite you?"

"Hell no! I've been doing this job for two decades now. I'm not going to let some varmints get the best of me. Unfortunately, I can't say the same for hunting dogs. I've seen coons chew up the best of hounds. Nasty buggers, nasty."

Z.Z. remembered that his uncle also would say, "It's a living," and repeated it.

"Cheers," he said and raised his can of beer. "I'm grateful to have you help around the farm while I'm at work—grateful as a strong cup of coffee with a shot of whiskey. I'm really thinking about your future. Your parents are back in Arizona, and you really don't want to work your dad's appliance shop there. I didn't either when I was your age. You bombed your first year of college. Nothing wrong with that. Back when I was around your age, I was dating girls in college, and they all said it was tough. What would you like to be doing in the future, after this farm season?"

The nephew shrugged. "I don't know. I honestly don't have a clue."

"Fair enough." Greybeard took several swallows of beer and threw the empty can to the far corner of the growing pile. "The reason I bring this all up is Fast Eddie is going to be retiring at the end of November. Retiring isn't the correct word, moving to Hawaii to work for another company is more accurate. He was with us ten years and was a terrific salesman. Anyway, I'm the assistant manager, and if you want the job, I'm sure Bob wouldn't object. He likes you a lot, too. They say opportunity knocks, but it has always been my experience that it whispers to you at a heavy metal concert. If you catch my meaning," he said with a wink.

"Opportunity knocks comes from the saying 'opportunity never knocks twice at any man's door.' But was shortened over the years."

"Is that a yes or a no, college boy?" Greybeard said with another wink.

"I don't know. Can I think about it?"

"Think about it, if you like. I like you, even though that goofy handlebar mustache of yours makes you look like a cartoon villain. You should try to grow it out like my beard." He laughed. "But people like you, and that's the key to success in this business."

At that moment, from the south side of the house, there were several loud bangs in a row.

The pest control man sighed. "Larry, I think one of the cellar doors isn't fully shut. Can you shut it?"

"Huh, what?" Lizard said, rubbing his eyes and sitting up from his crawled-up position.

The banging got louder.

"I better go down in the cellar and shut the storm doors," Lizard said, getting off the sofa. He grabbed his raincoat and hat but could only find one of his work gloves, so he put it on.

Larry, a.k.a. Lizard, unlocked the cellar door; it was made of corrugated old and rusty, and the hinges screeched when it swung open.

The cellar entrance was thick with spiderwebs, so he decided to turn on his flashlight.

The corrugated metal cellar slammed open and shut. The red rain splattered the walls by the entrance, and it seemed like they were bleeding, which creeped out Lizard.

He pushed a few of the webs away.

Strong winds blew against the cellar doors as the pummeling rainstorm continued.

Larry grabbed the door to shut it and felt a sharp pain, like he'd just been stung by a hornet or wasp. He jerked his hand back from the door handle and shined his flashlight on it. There was a red welt on the back of his palm, and it hurt like hell.

The cellar door swung open again, and red rain poured all over Lizard's hand. He screamed in pain.

Chapter Thirteen

July 10th
6:17 p.m.

After they finished their crack pipes, Viper walked toward the edge of the barn doors and watched the falling red rain. It looked like a rainstorm on Mars. Grizzly walked over to Honey, who was sitting on a hay bale.

"Let's screw," Grizzly whispered in Honey's ear, kissing her earlobe.

"Not in front of Viper."

"Why not? You used to date him."

"I'm not going to give Viper a peep show. It's over between the two of us. Now I have you."

"He'll probably jerk off watching us anyway."

"Eww," she said.

He moved even closer to her and ran his hand down her back and gently squeezed her behind.

"Not here, not now. Not with him watching," she whispered.

"Okay. Let's go upstairs..." He pointed to the hayloft. "...for more privacy."

Greybeard stood by Larry as he put his hand in the sink. Lizard's right hand had a wound about two inches wide and two inches long. The pest control tech was getting ready to turn on the water when Z.Z. said, "No!"

"Why?" Greybeard asked. "We have to clean the wound."

"If it was acid rain or some kind of chemical that caused this, water could spread it even more," Zach commented.

"What kind of burn is it?"

"I'm not sure it is a chemical burn. It looks like the skin was eaten away. Very strange. Wait—"

Z.Z. grabbed a magnified glass to get a better look.

Some of the slimy red spots on Lizard's wrist moved closer to Z.Z.'s wrist and crawled onto his skin.

The college dropout screamed. "Shit! It hurts." He grabbed the hose the family used to spray the dishes and blasted the red slime from his wrist with a jet of hot water. The slime fell off his hand and onto the basin of the sink.

Z.Z. sprayed the rest of the slime off Lizard's wrist, and it fell into the sink.

"What the hell?" Zach said, pointing at the slime slithering around in the sink. He kept spraying it with the hot water until it crawled into the garbage disposal. He put the plastic lid over the drain hole and hit the "start" button, which made a grinding noise for several moments before he turned it off.

"Whatever it is, it doesn't like hot steaming water. Do you have any bandages to wrap Lizard's wounds?"

"Yeah, below the sink," Greybeard said, opening the cabinet. The pest control man was an expert on both mold and fungi, but he'd never seen anything like this before.

"Are we going to take Lizard to the hospital?" Z.Z. asked.

Greybeard said, "We aren't going to the hospital. We're going to Big Bob's Bug Busters after it stops raining."

Chapter Fourteen

July 10th
6:29 p.m.

Mick "Viper" Weinhold tried to concentrate and listen to the rain pelting down on the barn's roof. But all he could focus on was what Jennifer "Honey" Wellington and Harry "Grizzly" Gerlach were doing up in the hayloft.

Mick could probably ignore it all if he hadn't slept with Jennifer before. He and Jen had both been hired by the Rosen Medical Supply Warehouse in Cicero around the same time. He learned that she also rode and invited her to join the Rattler MC. Shortly after that, they started dating, and all the dates ended the same—with Jen on her back, legs high in the air as he thrust as hard as he could.

All good things come to an end, though, especially when a nosy co-worker informed Jen that Mick was still sleeping with his ex.

Around that time, Harry was hired at Rosen's, and Jen started going out with him.

She nudged Mick into letting Harry join the MC, too.

Mick liked Harry. He was a hell of a nice enough guy and a better motorcycle mechanic than he was. He did, however, resent that Jen was sleeping with Harry instead of him. She was once his and should be again someday, he thought of someday offing Harry, but the guy was as tough as his bear nickname.

He was thinking of seeing if there was any rock left to smoke when a jeep stopped across the road.

Chapter Fifteen

July 10ᵗʰ
6:33 p.m.

Mark Neumann pulled the jeep to the side of the road in front of the derelict Baumann barn on the edge of town. The city had been talking about tearing it down for years, but for whatever reason, it always got voted down because of the sentimental local history of the place. While the volunteer fire department always lectured about it being a fire hazard, hometown nostalgia always won out.

It was almost impossible to see through the red rain anymore. Even with his wipers on high, he could barely see more than a few feet in front of him, and that's what made it so infuriating, since he was almost there. He would just have to drive on 270 until South Park Road, past the PDQ and Park View Diner, which had been closed for a few months, turn onto Montgomery Street and drive to the end of the road, and he'd be home.

Home Sweet Home. Zoey didn't have to work tomorrow, so he might even get lucky, and then it would be sweet, real sweet. He liked banging his boss, Sarah, and there was his co-worker, Alicia, and even a few of his clients. But it was good to get back to the wifey again.

As he drove, he noticed all the houses were dark. Probably a power outage, he thought. His chances of getting lucky now started to seem more remote. His stepdaughter and wife were probably sleeping on the couch.

And to make matters worse, he heard a weird noise coming from inside the car. There was a roundish box on the floor near the passenger seat. He examined it and thought it might be a cake box, but it was too small for that. He hadn't seen that box when he left in the morning for work. Maybe Zoey dropped it off. She was always doing stuff like that and telling him after the fact.

He looked at the box again, scratched his head, still no idea of what it was.

Then it hit him. It was a hat box. He had seen one many years ago in his grandma's attic.

How strange. Mark wasn't sure if Zoey had a hat box—or even hats—and wasn't sure why it was on the floor of the car, and even stranger yet, it had some holes on the top. Gingerly, he opened the box. It was dark inside the jeep, but he could make out something inside the box, and it wasn't a hat. It was something coiled, which quickly uncoiled, and he recognized it as a snake, a rattlesnake. The snake shook its rattle before striking and biting him on the hand.

Mark screamed as he tried to pull the snake off his hand, causing the snake to sink its fangs even deeper. He grabbed the door handle and jumped outside in the deluge red rain.

Viper was trying to make out why some guy ran out of his car screaming, but it was hard to see with all the red rain.

At this point, Grizzly and Honey came down the stairs. He was adjusting his zipper, and she was brushing her hair. They watched the man writhing on the ground with a rattlesnake attached to his hand, which was ironic considering the MC was named Rattlers.

As more rain hit him, the more he screamed and more and more skin and flesh disappeared from both. Their flesh was dissolving in the rain, leaving both bloody skeletons lying on the ground.

At this point, Viper slowly backed up in the barn, going further and further into the darkness.

"What do you make of that, Viper?" Grizzly asked. When he got no reply, he noticed that his fellow biker was nowhere to be found, which was strange. He caught a sudden movement from the corner of his eye. It looked like the other Rattler member was in the back of the barn, and he was running toward them out of the darkness.

"Viper?" Grizzly said one more time.

Viper was hiding in the darkness and, like the rattlesnake, made a surprise strike. Running from the back to the front, he did a dropkick onto Grizzly, who wasn't expecting it. Grizzly went flying forward onto the ground just a few feet from where the bloody remains of the man and the snake were.

As his flesh sizzled, Grizzly screamed. He tried to get up but was in too much pain, so he tried to crawl back to the barn but didn't make it. His skin and flesh melted away.

PART THREE:
RED SLIME

The rain had finally stopped. It was quiet and peaceful, but that didn't last long, as a dozen meteorites crashed into various sites around town. One even smashed into the side of the water tower, flooding the baseball field below where the Pelicans and Lumber-Kings had played earlier.

After that, an eerie, red fog engulfed Park View, making it impossible to see more than a few feet. But that wasn't the worst of it. The individual red raindrops agglutinated, thus creating red slime or slimy, red blobs that were hungry for human flesh.

Chapter Sixteen

July 10th
6:37 p.m.

Josie Lamberson screamed when the lights went out at the PDQ.

"It's okay," Brad Haskell said, trying to calm her down.

"That freaked me out," she said.

"At least no customers are in the store," he said.

As his eyes adjusted to the darkness, he made his way to the front doors and locked them.

"We don't want any customers wandering in here in the dark."

"Good idea."

"I know I am not supposed to be behind the counter when I'm not working. Since there is no electric, I won't be caught on camera. Are you okay?"

"Yeah," she said in a hushed voice.

A car pulled into the PDQ driveway, saw the lights were off, and drove away.

"I should put up a sign saying we're temporarily closed," he said.

"Good idea."

She walked over to the front counter drawer, took out a flashlight and wrote "CLOSED DUE TO WEATHER" on a sheet of paper with a marker and taped it to the front door.

"Can you do me a favor, Hon," Josie said in the sweetest voice she could muster.

"What's that?" Brad said.

"Could you toss all the trash in the dumpster out back?"

He swallowed the last of his root beer, then tossed the plastic bottle into the nearest trash can. "Sure, no problem."

After a few moments of silence, Josie asked, "Did you walk here?"

"Yeah."

"I'll give you a ride home after we close up."

"Thanks."

Chapter Seventeen

July 10^{*th*}
6:37 p.m.

There were screams and more screams and then silence.

Honey lay on the barn floor, crying, her arms reaching out for Grizzly, who was nothing more than a bloody pulp outside in the rain.

"Why? Why did you do that?" Honey said between sobs.

Viper didn't answer her; instead, he circled around Honey and put his hands on her thighs.

"Get your hands off of me." Honey wiggled out of his grasp. "I will touch you anywhere I want now that Grizzly's gone," Viper said, looking down at her.

She stood up and stepped back. She grabbed her switchblade out of her back pocket and flicked the switch. "If you touch me again, I'll cut you."

"Is that so?" Viper said, stepping slowly in her direction. "I like a challenge. I wanted you for so long, and now I can finally have you without Grizzly around to interfere."

Honey slowly walked backward. Viper moved toward her.

"I'm warning you," Honey said, tears running down her face.

The biker took two quick steps toward her, his hand outstretched to grab her. She quickly cut him with the knife, the blade slicing the top of his wrist.

Viper screamed out in pain. His hand was covered in blood. "You bitch!" He advanced toward her again.

She swung the blade in his direction and took a step backward, not seeing the rake lying in the hay. The rake's wooden handle flung against her back, causing her to wince in pain. Viper moved quickly, snatching the switchblade from her hand.

He pointed the knife at her. "You are going to pay for cutting me—with your body."

Before he could finish the sentence, she turned and climbed the wooden steps to the hayloft as fast as she could. Viper was behind her by three or four steps. When he reached the top step, Honey kicked him with her left leg, booting him in the face. He lost his balance and fell to the hay-covered wooden floor.

She saw him rise and hurl himself toward the steps.

He stopped before reaching the top step and looked around before advancing. A pitchfork missed his face by inches. He went down a few steps and then started climbing again; this time, the pitchfork almost touched his eye. He descended the steps. When he reached the floor, he had an idea. He should be up for hours because of the crack. She would eventually fall asleep, and then he would get her.

Chapter Eighteen

July 10th
6:45 p.m.

A red fog surrounded the barn. Visibility was limited to a few feet. An eerie red glow was shining in the distance, but nobody seemed to know what the source of the glow was.

Trying to find a place to rest against the wall, a nail ripped most of her crop top. Half of her right breast was exposed. She had a tattoo above her chest, featuring a grinning Cheshire Cat from *Alice in Wonderland* with the words, "When you can't look on the bright side, I will sit with you in the dark."

She had fallen asleep and awakened when she heard a creak. She noticed that it had finally stopped raining. She heard another creaking noise.

She looked over at the steps and saw Viper slowly climbing. He reached the last step. She grabbed the pitchfork, but Viper grabbed it, too. They struggled, and Honey lost her balance and fell; she knocked him off the steps. They both plummeted to the floor, landing hard on the hay-scattered floor.

Honey felt dizzy as she tried to get up. It was too late because Viper clambered on top of her, pinning her to the ground.

"Take off your clothes."

"No."

"Take off your clothes. Now!" He reached into his pants, pulled out the switchblade, and opened the blade. "Okay, I'm going to have to cut them off of you instead—"

"No! I'll do what you want. I can't move. You're on top of me."

"Okay," he said, getting up and off her.

She brushed the hay off her clothes and put her hand on the edge of her top, acting as if she was taking it off, but instead she grabbed the pitchfork. That took Viper by surprise, and she seized the moment by violently stabbing him in the stomach with the pitchfork twice.

He fell to the floor, bleeding in the straw and grunting in pain. He tried to stand, but the pain was unbearable.

Jen threw on her jacket, pushed her motorcycle outside, and, taking one last look at the bloody, skeletal remains of Grizzly, started the bike in frantic haste, and headed out into the red fog. It was hard to see. She was driving recklessly, not knowing where she was going. She'd rather take the chance of running into a tree or car than encountering the biker again.

Viper knew he shouldn't, but he yanked the pitchfork out of his gut. Screaming in agony, he tossed it aside and got to his feet. Trying to staunch the gushes of blood, he knew he should go to the hospital, but he was determined to make Honey pay for what she did. He hobbled over to his motorcycle, got on, and started it, then drove out into the crimson fog.

Zoey put the key into the ignition and was ready to turn it when she saw something unusual on the hood of her SUV. It was hard to make out what it was in the dark. She studied it a little longer and then realized what it was—the distributor cap. That made a lot more sense now. That's why it took the escaped convict so long to go from the garage to inside the house. Then she heard a groan and knew it was coming from inside the freezer. The Butcher had awakened.

"Sophie, I'm going to get the wheelchair, and you're going to get out of here as fast as you can," Zoey said. "You understand?"

Her daughter nodded.

She quietly took the wheelchair from the back and put her daughter in it.

Sophie wheeled out of the garage and into the red fog.

She ran back into the garage and grabbed the wooden bat from the SUV, then hid beside the refrigerator, adjacent to the freezer.

McKenzie sat on a bench with her head slumped down, her legs pulled up, and her arms wrapped around them to keep herself warm from the red rain outside the shelter she was now trapped in.

She tried to call her parents but had no cell reception.

The power went out, and all the houses went dark.

Storms don't last forever, but this one seemed like it did. The scarlet raindrops hitting everything looked like a bloody battlefield after a war.

She sat listening to the rain fall and fall; it had a pattern to it. Not soothing, but more unnerving, like desolation and isolation engulfing the town.

Little by little, it seemed like it was slowing down.

And then it stopped.

She listened for a few moments; she heard a few drops of rain falling from the trees, but there was no longer red rain coming down from the sky.

Her moment of triumph was followed by more dread.

The red fog replaced the red rain and crept over the ground; it was impossible to see beyond a few feet. The crimson mist was as thick as an old jar of molasses.

She heard the truck's door open and the annoying doorbell dinging to let the driver know that the door was open.

"McKenzie?" Doug shouted. He couldn't see very far in front of him. The shelter was about twenty or thirty feet in front of the truck, and he had taken a lot more steps than that. Then he realized he was still on the street; he wasn't even on the grass.

"Doug, I'm over here," she said.

"Where?"

"Here?"

"Where?"

"Over here."

Doug realized he wasn't near his truck anymore. The hazy moonlight and the red mist made it hard to gauge his surroundings. To make matters worse, there was a creature in the fog growling at him.

"I think there's an angry dog near me, near me," Doug said. "You are studying to be a vet; what should I do?"

"Stop moving," McKenzie said. "Avoid eye contact."

"I can hardly see it." Doug stopped moving and squinted to get a better look at the creature. "It is a wolf. A goddamn wolf!"

"Wolf. Wolf? There are no wolves in Iowa. It's probably a coyote. They're scavengers. They don't attack."

"It's growling at me; I am sure it is a wolf."

"It's probably a mommy coyote guarding her young."

"The fog is so thick I can't see more than a couple of feet in front of me," he said, panicking. "And the growls are getting louder."

"It isn't a wolf. You gotta trust me on this, Doug," she said. "Slowly back away."

Doug turned in the other direction and started slowly walking backward, then saw another coyote circling him. That one followed yet another, which followed the other two. "There are two more right next to it, and they are growling at me."

"Like I said, a mother and her cubs."

"No, they're all adults, maybe five or six of them now."

"Coyotes don't travel in packs."

"Wolves do."

"I told you... There are no wolves—"

Before she could finish her sentence, McKenzie heard screams. None of this made any sense to her unless they weren't coyotes but a pack of wild dogs or something else. McKenzie tried to run, but she couldn't see where she was going until she stumbled against a picnic bench. Then her left leg hit one of the metal pillars.

She fell to the ground; the pain raced up her leg. She held her leg for several moments as the red fog engulfed her.

McKenzie slowly got up. The pain still throbbed in her left leg, so she walked slowly, her hands feeling in front of her as if she were playing Blind Man's Bluff and trying not to hit anything else.

Hearing the dinging of the open door on the truck, she walked slowly in that direction. She almost ran into the bumper. She put her hands on the hood of the truck and followed it around until she came upon the open door. After she slid inside and closed the door, the dinging finally stopped.

She started the truck, reversed, then turned left onto the asphalt road. She turned on the headlights, but because of the dense fog, the high beams didn't shine through but reflected into her eyes, making it almost impossible to see. She turned on the low beams and drove very slowly, squinting, trying to find Doug.

She drove the truck slowly and saw a coyote in her headlights. It had blood all over its muzzle. She stepped on the brake, grabbed the tire iron that was lying on the floor, and got out of the truck.

She slowly walked backward; the coyotes were coming from the same direction as the truck, so she couldn't run there. Instead, she turned around and ran as fast as she could, hoping she wouldn't run into one of the columns holding up the shelter. Finally, she made it to the cold cement flooring and leaped on top of the picnic tables.

The coyotes followed her. When they arrived at the picnic table, they circled around it, growling even louder. One leapt tried to table on to the table, but she kicked the beast in the head, it yelped in pain and fell off onto the concrete floor.

Travis was in pain, but he slowly got up and swung the bathroom door open. The door leading to the garage was open. was still a little wobbly. He put his hand on his head and removed it; it was covered with blood. He wiped the blood on his jumpsuit.

"Come out, come out where everywhere you are." He took a few steps. "Where are we hiding, my pretty?"

"Here!" Zoey leaped from beside the freezer and swung the wooden bat at his head, hitting multiple times. Travis stumbled, then fell back onto the garage floor covered in blood.

She ran out of the garage, searching for her daughter and yelling, "Sophie! Sophie!"

Chapter Nineteen

July 10th
7:00 p.m.

The comedian flicked his headlights on and off.

The black minister stepped out of the doorway of Park View Pentecostal Church and shouted, "The rain has stopped. It should be safe for you to come in."

Uncle Brew and El Mago got out of the car, but the short distance from the street to the church was next to impossible to see through, like looking through pea soup with extra crumbled crackers in it.

"I can't see you or the church," Uncle Brew said.

"Me, either," the magician replied.

"That's okay. I'll sing one of our hymns. Just follow my voice. I sing it loud every week in church, so you ought to be able to hear my voice." He paused for a moment, then began to sing:

> "Rock of Ages, cleft for me,
> Let me hide myself in Thee;
> Let the water and the blood..."

The minister had a lovely voice, but more importantly, it was loud; like a beacon, it guided the comedian and magician to their destiny.

He held out his hand, "Pastor Matthew Bell."

"Uncle Brew," he said, shaking the pastor's hand.

"El Mago."

"Come inside. It might not be much, but it beats this creepy red fog," the minister said. "We have a new church organ, an old roof that leaks, but it's still our home."

Everyone walked through the doors.

"It looks like one of those one-class school rooms," El Mago said.

It looked like a school, but instead of desks, there were chairs. Instead of a chalkboard, there was a stage and pulpit.

"It was at one time. Built in the late eighteen hundreds."

"Wow," Uncle Brew chimed in.

"The school bell still works. We use it, of course, to ring for Sunday services."

Uncle Brew stopped in his tracks. "I bet it's loud."

"Rumor is, you can hear the bell ring all through Park View," the religious man stated.

"I have an idea," Uncle Brew said. "You should ring the bell, keep ringing it, and maybe people from around the city will come here for safety."

The pastor scratched his grayish beard and said, "That's a great idea."

Honey was driving the motorcycle as fast as she dared. With the red fog everywhere, she could hardly see where she was going. She was worried the road wouldn't remain straight forever and she'd end up crashed in some ditch, so she slowed down.

There was a fork in the road. But Honey couldn't really tell that it was, was just guessing because the road changed. She decided to get on the other road instead, probably used by teenagers with their dirt bikes.

The road she was on before continued onto a covered bridge.

Then she heard Viper's motorcycle. He was following her. She couldn't see the bike, but she could hear it; it wasn't too far away.

She went down the dirt road further, the fog grew more intense. There might be a chance Viper would see the motorcycle taillight and hear the motor. She turned the bike off and pushed it.

Josie Lamberson took her flashlight, turned it on, and shined the beam on the floors and aisles as she walked to the ladies' bathroom. Once inside, she pulled her skirt up and her thong down as she sat on the toilet.

When she finished, she flushed the toilet, washed and dried her hands, then flipped the toilet lid down and sat on it to contemplate her situation for a few moments.

"To screw or not to screw, that is the question," she said, paraphrasing Shakespeare's *MacBeth* if he was off-color.

Screwing a co-worker always led to trouble, and sleeping with someone a lot younger always seemed to fizzle, too.

But the dating world had turned into a battlefield in the last few years. Competition was fierce and cutthroat at that:

Co-eds wore skimpy clothes and even skimpier underwear.

Hot mamas wore yoga pants and spent more time in the gym than in the kitchen.

There were dating sites, but it seemed they attracted freaks, geeks, losers, and those that no one wanted to date.

Josie sighed; she decided to be just friends with her coworker.

Pastor Matthew Bell kept ringing the church bell. A fire truck slowly went down the road, the light from the emergency vehicle leading the way for an old Ford and a couple other cars.

More vehicles pulled into the church parking lot. The sound of the bell was beckoning them.

The roof was in need of repair, and the red slime was leaking into the bell tower, too.

He saw something out of the corner of his eye and turned around to get a better look. He stopped ringing the bell. What he saw took his breath away—literally. He couldn't breathe from watching the horror. The walls and ceiling were all red. It wasn't blood; it was the red slime—and to make matters worse, the slime was dripping down the walls toward him.

He walked to the stairwell, but there was red slime everywhere, and it kept sliding closer and closer to him.

"Have no fear, Greybeard is here," the pastor heard from below the stairs.

He heard multiple footsteps running up the stairs.

He saw Greybeard, and behind him were his son, Lizard, and nephew, Zach. All three were carrying power steamers. They reminded him of the trio from the *Ghostbusters* film, only not as cool. They started blasting the red slime with the hot steam, and every time the steam hit the slime, it vaporized into nothingness. Soon, there was no slime left.

After all the slime had been cleared, Greybeard spoke. "Lizard, stay up here to make sure no more slime tries to slide in through the leaky roof. Me and ZZ are going to comb the basement."

Chapter Twenty

July 10th
7:15 p.m.

Travis tried to get up, but he was in too much pain to move. He was lying on the garage floor, covered in his own blood. His head was killing him. It felt like Lizzy Borden had whacked her ax on his head multiple times. To make matters even worse, all the blood dripping into his eyes made it even harder to see. He did see a small creature running towards him. He thought it might be a hamster who might have got lost in the house and somehow ended up in the garage and was crawling toward him. He tried to focus, but his vision was impaired. He tried once again to make sense of his surroundings.

To his horror, he realized it wasn't a hamster by his head, but a rat. The rat wasn't alone. He saw the driveway through the open garage door. The rats were crawling out of the sewer and up the driveway and into the garage there were hundreds of rats, and they were hungry, hungry for flesh and blood. He tried to scream, but the rats jumped on him and started devouring him.

Dana "Pinky" Kincaid thought she heard what might have been screams coming from next door. That would be the Neumann place—Zoey, Mark, and Sophie. She used to babysit Sophie when she was younger and always liked Zoey. Mark, on the other hand, always stared at her, making her feel uncomfortable, but she tried to be civil toward him nevertheless. When he offered her a ride home, she always said, "I live across the street."

The last few days, she had barely been able to get off the couch because her life had come crashing down all around her. For the last few weeks, she had been trying to pick up all the pieces again, but she just hadn't been able to.

It all started when she was laid off from her job at the Davenport Supermarket Superstore. Pinky had been working there since she was 16 years old. After she graduated from high school, she worked there full-time. Now, at 22, she was unemployed and not sure what to do. She knew she couldn't afford to live in her apartment anymore and had to move back home.

Two days after she moved back to her childhood home, her parents decided to visit some friends in Florida. Since going to the Sunshine State, she only got one text from her mom saying they were going to stay for two weeks or more. She suspected the trip South was to avoid her, she never got along with her folks.

The next day, her Jeep Grand Cherokee was impounded. She had fallen several months behind on the car payments because of credit card debt. A tow truck had towed the Jeep away in the middle of the night.

Then her boyfriend broke up with her. Losing her job, apartment, jeep, and boyfriend in such a short time, Pinky melted down. All her energy was zapped and drained and blended into the sofa. She only got up to go to the bathroom or the fridge to get something to eat.

She tried to watch TV, but the reality shows were not real enough for her, and the sitcoms weren't that funny. Then the power went off.

She was sitting in the dark for what seemed like a long time. Then she heard what was like a slurping sound coming outside the window, like some teenager sucking on their straw for the last few drops of their drink.

The sound got louder.

She grabbed a flashlight she kept on the end table and flashed the beam around the room. When the light hit the window, she saw it was covered with red slime, which was pulsating against the pane, trying to get inside.

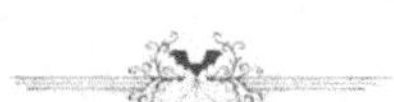

The church was packed. Greybeard stood in front of a chalkboard with a drawing of Park View marked with: "Zone: A," "Zone: B," and "Zone: C."

Greybeard said, "Everyone knows which group they are in?"

The crowd murmured that they did.

"Good," the man with the long, gray beard said. "We only have nine power steamers, so each group gets three units. Group A, I want you to start at Scott County Park and work back to the P.D.Q. If you see any slimy, red blobs, blast them to hell. Group B, I want you to hit the East side of Park View and work back to the P.D.Q., and Group C, I want you to hit the West side of Park View and work to the P.D.Q. Any questions?"

"Yeah, how long do these things stay hot?" The retired wrestler, Toxic Frankenstein, was wearing a Frankenstein mask and his clothes were all black.

"About an hour or so, or until it runs out of steam," Greybeard answered.

"What is this red blob-ish stuff?" Brandon Ruok, the police officer, asked.

"I have no idea," Greybeard answered. "If it gets on your flesh, it'll eat it away. Any other questions?"

More murmuring but no questions.

"Good," Greybeard said. "Good luck and Godspeed. Try to meet back at the P.D.Q. in about an hour."

Honey kept pushing her bike along the dirt road, and Viper's motorcycle could still be heard in the distance.

He kept going straight on the road onto the covered bridge. In the middle of the bridge, he lost traction, the bike slid, and he fell to the pavement. All he could see was red, red everywhere. The red slime was crawling toward him. As he moved to pick up his hog, he found red slime covered it. As soon as he touched the cycle, the red slime slipped onto his fingertips and speedily ate away the flesh, moving quickly along his hands, arms...

Viper screamed, but the screams didn't last long as the red slime devoured him to the bone, leaving a red, pulpy skeleton on the bridge.

Honey smirked when she heard the screams. The victory was fleeting. As she pushed the bike out of the puddle she had stepped in, she realized it was red slime. Red slime was all over her boots. It crawled up her legs and thighs, eating away her flesh. She screamed uselessly into the red fog.

The police officer, Brandon, and his little convoy consisted of Charlie Hiaasen, a retired farmer who drove a beat-up truck; Katie Wright, the former owner of the Ice Cream Palace who now worked as a banker in Davenport, drove a 2017 silver Chrysler Pacific; Ramsey Blackwell, driving a street cleaner with bright, almost blinding, flashing orange lights; and Uncle Brew and El Mago in their 1999 Mercury Grand Marquis Station Wagon, with Pastor Bell sitting in the back seat, a Bible in his lap.

Brandon drove his police car in front of a shelter and turned on his spotlight. It sounded like he just ran over a dead animal in the middle of the road. He stopped the car, took out his flashlight, and, playing the beam across the road, he saw he had run over the mangled remains of a teenager. He heard a noise; it was the growling of angry animals. He pointed his flashlight in that direction and saw the coyotes circling a teenager trapped on a picnic table.

The police officer said, "Everybody, stay back. This could be very dangerous." He jumped out of the car with his handgun, a Glock 22. He fired all fifteen rounds into the coyotes; they all fell to the ground dead.

McKenzie jumped off the table and ran out of the shelter. When she was outside the shelter, she heard a rumbling noise and looked up. The roof was covered in red slime and had transformed into a reddish blob that fell off the roof and onto the police officer.

Katie, the minivan mama, was the closest to the shelter. She jumped out of her vehicle with a steamer and started blasting the red slime off the police officer. But it was too late. His flesh had already been stripped to the bones.

Sophie wheeled her wheelchair as fast as she could. She was scared. It was dark, and the thick, red fog made it impossible to see more than a couple of feet in front of her. She knew she was on Park Lane Circle but couldn't tell if the next street was Cherokee Drive or South Park View Drive. She would wheel as fast as she could and hope for the best. It was neither street; instead, it was Concord Court, the dead-end sign telling her she made the wrong choice. She spun the wheelchair around, ready to go back, but it was too late. A reddish slime blob was practically on top of her. She was trapped. She was hot, tired, and sweaty. With all the breath she could muster, she screamed at the top of her lungs.

At first, she thought it must be her imagination, but she saw the Frankenstein monster blasting hot steam at the red slime, vaporizing it. Then she recognized the monster. It was Toxic Frankenstein, her wrestling idol.

Toxic Frankenstein dissolved all the slime in the area and ran over to her. "We got to get you out of here. It isn't safe."

"What about my mom?"

"How far is she?"

"About eight blocks."

Toxic Frankenstein thought about it for a moment. "We're all supposed to meet back at the P.D.Q. It's only a couple of blocks away. After that, I will go back to get your mom."

"Okay."

"I'll push you; you look tired. We don't have much time. There's even more slime in the East Side of town."

He gave her the steamer.

"Hold this and hold on tight." He grabbed hold of the wheelchair and shoved forward.

Dana heard a loud noise rumbling from the fireplace. She looked at it. It sounded as if Santa Claus were stuck coming down the chimney and decided to use a sledgehammer to get out.

She looked up at the fireplace chimney. She didn't see Saint Nick. Instead, she saw a red, slimy blob sliding down.

She turned the knob to close the damper, the metal doors that closed off the chimney from the fireplace. The red slime slipped through the metal doors and approached her relentlessly.

Dana couldn't go out the door or windows because they were covered in slime. She had an idea: She'd go upstairs and climb onto the balcony; maybe a fire truck or a helicopter would see her and help her.

She ran upstairs and rushed through the terrace doors. Immediately, she knew she had made a mistake. The roof and the walls of the house were covered in slime, and it dripped onto her. Dana's screams went unheard. The red slime covered her in a matter of seconds, leaving a red, glistening skeleton.

Brad took the bags of trash to the dumpster behind the PDQ. As dark as it was outside, he didn't see the steel doors to the trash compactor were covered with slime. "What the hell?" The red sludge started devouring his flesh. He screamed, dropped the trash bags, then jumped back in pain. At the same time, he heard a rumbling noise from above. The rain gutters above him were shaking like an earthquake as they broke away from the side of the building, flooding the area with crimson ooze.

It happened so fast that Brad didn't even have a chance to scream. In a matter of a few moments, he was reduced to crimson-stained bones.

Josie came around the corner to see what the commotion was. She saw the fallen gutter, the skeletal remains of Brad, and, worst of all, a red blob creeping toward her. She turned and saw more slime approaching her. She was surrounded.

Jumping to the window's edge under the awning. She above the ground but the red slime was sliding up and down the building.

She heard a noise; it grew steadily louder. From her angle and the fog, she couldn't really make out who it was. Someone jumped out of the vehicle and sprayed something at the slime, vaporizing it immediately.

"Josie? Is that you?" a voice asked.

"Yeah."

"It's Zach Zobeck. Z.Z. You used to babysit me when I was a kid."

"Oh. Z.Z. Can you help me?"

"It's not really that high, but if you fall, I will catch you." He put his arms under the lower back and rear. "Slide down."

She slid from the window ledge and dropped to the sidewalk.

Z.Z. braced himself, held out his arms, and caught her awkwardly. The impact of the fall almost knocked him over. He grunted as he lowered her to the ground. He noticed she had her eyes closed during the jump. "You can open your eyes now. You are safe."

"Jesus! You just saved my life," Josie said breathlessly.

"I'm glad you are all right. But I'm sorry."

"For saving my life?"

"Oh, that's nothing," he said. "I just sprayed the hell out of the red slime and helped you get down."

They both heard a loud noise that sounded like running feet and wheels. When they looked to the parking lot, they saw Toxic Frankenstein pushing Sophie's wheelchair onto the handicap-accessible ramp.

"You guys made it," Zach said happily.

"Sophie! Sophie!"

Everyone turned. Zoey was running down the street as fast as she could. She ran up to her daughter and hugged her so tight that she almost pulled her out of the wheelchair.

Suddenly, the hazy red moon disappeared behind dark, reddish clouds.

Sophie had a somber look on her face as she said, "It's going to rain again."

"What?" Josie asked.

Z.Z. grabbed Josie's hand, "Go inside. Now!" He grabbed the doors and flung them open. Josie ran in, followed by Toxic Frankenstein, Zoey pushing Sophie.

Once inside, Zach closed the doors.

A single raindrop fell. Then another and another and another. Everyone looked through the open door as the rain grew heavier and heavier. The red rain had returned once again.

ABOUT THE AUTHORS

Terrie Leigh Relf, an active member of the HWA and a lifetime member of the SFPA, has been on staff at various independent presses over the decades. Currently, she is with Hiraeth Publishing, where she hosts the somewhat quarterly drabble contest, serves as the lead editor for *Hungur Chronicles,* and works on a variety of special projects. In addition to Hiraeth Publishing, Relf is the poetry editor for *Tales from the Moonlit Path.* She also facilitates a writers' group as well as a networking group for writers, editors, and publishers. Relf teaches English at National University and is an integrative life coach, writing coach, and Reiki Master. She is currently working on *Beacon Lights of Ranat,* the third book in one of her trilogies.

Michael McCarty has been a professional writer since 1983 and is the author of over fifty books of fiction and nonfiction. His nonfiction includes *Ghostly Tales of Route 66* (co-written with Connie Corcoran Wilson), *Ghosts of the Quad Cities* (with Mark McLaughlin), *Eerie Quad Cities* (with John Brassard Jr.), the mega books of interviews *Modern Mythmakers: 35 Interviews with Horror and Science Fiction Writers and Filmmakers* and *More Modern Mythmakers,* which features interviews with Ray Bradbury, Dean Koontz, John Carpenter, Richard Matheson, Elvira, Linnea Quigley, John Saul and many more.

His fiction includes *Frankenstein's Mistress: Tales of Love & Monsters*; *Dracula Transformed and Other Bloodthirsty Tales*; *Dark Duets*; *Dark Cities: Dark Tales*; *A Little Help from My Fiends*; *Liquid Diet & Midnight Snack*; *Lost Girl of the Lake*; *Biters: Tales of Zombies & Vampires*; and *I Kissed A Ghoul.*

Michael is a five-time Bram Stoker Finalist, and in 2008, he won the David R. Collins Literary Achievement Award from the Midwest Writing Center. He lives in Rock Island, Illinois, with his wife, Cindy, and pet rabbit, Yeti.

His blog site is http://monstermikeyaauthor.wordpress.com. Like his official Facebook page, http://www.facebook.com/michaelmccarty. horror, and the Official Ghosts of the Quad Cities Facebook Page: https://www.facebook. com/QCGhosts.

"Michael McCarty is given full rein, and off he goes on a bizarre trip of the imagination, all stops out, no limits, hell-for-leather," – William Nolan author of *Logan's Run*

This collection of horror and science fiction stories includes a sequel to Mary Shelley's *Frankenstein* – with Victor Frankenstein, the monster, and a blind fortune teller named Rose Blackthorn. In other tales... even the apocalypse won't stop Leonard Cartwright from searching for his wife in the ruins; after getting struck by lightning that left him in a coma for twenty years, Jackson Heyward awakens with the ability to talk to the dead; will the discovery of the power of invisibility help save Dr. Nick's failing relationship with his soulmate, or will it aid in its destruction? And many more twisted tales.

Sometimes love is a monster ...

And there is no escape from *Frankenstein's Mistress: Tales of Love & Monsters*.